79p

Pig's Progress

MORE PIGS, LESS PARSONS!
—Chartist placard, 1848

*"I spoke to the prophets, gave them many visions
and told parables through them."*
—Hosea 12:10, 8th c. BC

Pig's Progress

Jeanette Sears

with illustrations by Adela Slomski

Copyright © Jeanette Sears 2011

The moral right of Jeanette Sears to be identified as the Author of this Work has been asserted by her in accordance with the Copyright, Designs and Patents Act 1988.

First published in English by PiquantFiction in 2011—www.piqfic.com

PiquantFiction is an imprint of Piquant.

Piquant

PO Box 83, Carlisle, CA3 9GR, UK

ISBN 978-1903689-73-8

British Library Cataloguing in Publication Data

Sears, Jeanette.

  Pig's progress.

  1. Swine--Fiction. 2. Farm life--Fiction. 3. Liberty--
  Fiction. 4. Conduct of life--Fiction. 5. Parables.
  I. Title
  823.9'2-dc22

  ISBN-13: 9781903689738

This is a work of fiction. All characters, organizations, and events portrayed in this novel are either products of the author's imagination or are used fictitiously.

Illustrations © Adela Slomski 2010

Typesetting by To a Tee: www.2aT.com

Contents

I

The Pigs are Revolting!

Once upon a time there were Three Little Pigs ...
Actually, they weren't so little any more, and a pig
in puberty is a pig under stress. The not-so-little
pigs expressed this by growing rebellious.

'This sty isn't big enough!' said the first little pig, pushing
over part of the fence.

'This swill isn't hot enough!' said the second little pig,
kicking over one of the troughs.

'And what's worse, there's no entertainment!' said the
third little pig, who merely sat gazing into the distance in
discontent.

Life, the little pigs felt, had become very dull indeed. It was
obvious something drastic was needed to liven things up.

The real source of the problem, they decided, was the
Farmer who owned Far Off Farm where they lived. He was
responsible for all the silly rules and regulations about when
the animals should go to bed, what they were supposed to
eat, which of the other animals they were allowed to mix
with, etc, etc, etc.

The general feeling of frustration experienced by the little pigs came to a head in the autumn of that year.

It was harvest time, and all the animals had been driven to a large barn in the middle of Far Off Farm for the annual festival at which they had to recite the rules and regulations of the farm in unison.

It was an exercise the animals felt was designed to humiliate them. Having to salute the flag of Far Off Farm (a picture of a cow and plough sewn onto a pair of the milkmaid's polka-dot bloomers) as each animal paraded past it really was the last straw. Several of the animals were heard to mutter that the four-legged animals had an unfair advantage when it came to saluting. It was very embarrassing for the ducks, for example, to keel over in public each year because the hired hands who ran the farm had ruled that saluting with wings wasn't good enough – they had to use a foot. It was rumoured that the birds had decided to demand counselling after the parade to help any animals psychologically scarred by the experience. They were still scratching their heads over what to do about the fish, who had to come out of the water for the ceremony and hold their breath for at least five minutes.

However, one good thing about Far Off Farm's Rules and Regulations Recital Day was that the rest of the day was a holiday for all the animals on the farm.

The three little pigs spent the rest of that afternoon wandering contentedly around a field that was normally out of bounds. They were able to forage around the bushes and trees that marked the beginning of the Whispering Wood right on the edge of the farm. The wood didn't seem as frightening in daylight as it tended to look at night, and it was so far away from the little pigs' sty that just being there gave them a glorious feeling of freedom.

When they had had enough to eat (which was quite a few hours later), they all sat beneath the shade of a tree with their eyes closed and trotters folded over full, taut bellies.

'A few after-dinner truffles wouldn't go amiss,' said the first little pig, whose name was Parsnip.

'Some coffee dregs and potato peel wine would go down very nicely at this moment,' said the second little pig, whose name was Parsley.

'Mmm,' said the third little pig dreamily, whose name was Parsifal.

'Rip me off a root, Parsley,' said Parsnip, without bothering to move a muscle. 'I feel like an after-dinner smoke.'

'Rip one off yourself, you lazy pig,' retorted Parsley, who did not like being told what to do by her older brother.

'But you're nearer the bush than me. You can reach more easily.'

'No, I'm not.'

'Yes, you are.'

'No, I'm not!'

'Yes, you are!'

'Oh for goodness' sake, I'll get it,' said Parsifal. He was the youngest of the three, although only by minutes.

Parsifal heaved himself round onto his stomach, with a great deal of sighing and grunting, and slowly moved towards a bush to which pigs are particularly partial. He tunnelled a little way into the earth with one trotter and, with the help of another trotter and his teeth, he ripped off one of the bush's succulent roots. Hoping that Parsnip wouldn't see, he quickly chewed it and gulped it down.

Then, with a satisfied grin, he pulled off another root for his brother.

'Thanks,' said Parsnip. 'But don't dribble on it or it'll never light.'

With the skill that comes from years of practice, Parsnip struck a trotter against a stone, producing a spark, and lit the root. He then lay back against the tree with the root dangling from one side of his mouth and breathed in the smoke—though not without an initial fit of coughing.

'This farm is the pits,' said Parsley suddenly.

'Oh, I don't know,' said Parsnip. 'I'm sure it has potential, if only the right person were running it.'

'Like you, you mean?' snorted Parsley.

'Well, he couldn't do a much worse job than they're doing now,' said Parsifal. 'The farm is really going to seed. The Rules and Regulations Ceremony today was the worst ever. Getting the geese to sing the farm song instead of hiring a proper band was just cheap. I don't know who was more embarrassed—us or them. There was no way they were going to sound like a brass band!'

'It's the fish I feel sorry for,' said Parsley. 'They get the worst deal every year.'

'It's amphibianist,' said Parsnip. He yelped as some burning ash from the root fell onto his arm.

'It's what?' said the other two little pigs.

'It's amphib...eee...er, you should have listened the first time,' muttered Parsnip who, distracted by the pain in his arm, had forgotten the word already.

'You said 'am-fib-yon-istow,' said Parsifal helpfully. 'Is that one of your new words?'

Parsifal was referring to his older brother's habit of reading any bits of newspapers or magazines that he found lying around in rubbish heaps on the farm or shredded in their bedding. Parsnip was always trying to learn long, interesting-sounding words that he would drop into conversations, whether or not he knew their meanings. It was part of his 'How to Win Friends and Influence Animals' policy. Parsnip meant to get on in life.

'You should have listened the first time,' Parsnip repeated stubbornly. 'I don't see why I should have to repeat things for an ignorant pig.'

Parsifal shrugged his shoulders. 'Please yourself,' he said.

There was silence for a while. Parsnip chewed on his smouldering root, Parsley chewed the inside of her cheek, and Parsifal chewed over an idea.

'You know what we were saying about the Farm going to seed,' began Parsifal slowly.

'You mean what *you* were saying,' said Parsley in her older sister voice.

'Whatever,' said Parsifal. 'Well, I was thinking. Why don't we complain to the Farmer and get something done about it? You know all those rules and regulations we don't like? Can't we try and get them changed?'

'You mean like what sorts of pigs we're allowed to breed with?' asked Parsley, and immediately coughed and went very red. She didn't want her brothers to know she had been pondering this subject.

'Well, anything you like,' said Parsifal.

'That's an idea,' said Parsnip, beginning to get interested. He sat up. 'But has anybody ever seen the Farmer? I mean the real one? Didn't he leave the farm a long time ago?'

'Yes, and left us in the care of those rotten hired hands,' snorted Parsley.

'They certainly don't seem to care much about the upkeep of the farm,' said Parsifal. 'I'm sure I've often heard singing in the farmhouse at night that sounds, well ... like Dad used to when he'd had a bit too much parsnip wine.'

The boar had held it close to him the whole night long

The little pigs giggled. They had often been told that their father, a majestic boar, had been very merry on parsnip wine on the night they were born. As they sat together in the sun, their minds drifted back to the familiar story.

It had been their father's task to pick names for the piglets while his wife recovered from the birth. He had thus (between hiccups) named the first piglet of the litter 'Parsshhnipp.' (Hic!) 'Sorry, *Parsnip*—after the wine.' It had made sense for him to carry on in the same vein, so he called the second piglet Parsley (after his favourite herb).

But then came tragedy. All the other little piglets in the litter died moments after birth. The only other survivor was a tiny scrap of a thing that could hardly draw breath. The boar had held it close to him the whole night long, so it could feel the warmth of his body. He had prayed that it would live and that the hired hands would not drown it in the river the next morning. That was what usually happened to the runt of any litter. The hired hands didn't want to waste food on a weak piglet that would probably die anyway. They said it wasn't 'commercially viable'. The boar didn't understand these words, but he knew what they meant in practise. His son would be killed because he was small.

So the boar had hidden the third piglet while he grew bigger and stronger, and the mother pig, the sow, had nursed him faithfully. For a few nights it was touch-and-go, but within three weeks it was clear that the third little pig was going to live. The mother and father celebrated with a bit more parsnip wine (fermented in a trough kept especially for the purpose). It felt so good to have triplets.

'Now that we know he's going to live, he needs a name,' said the boar.

'Actually,' said the sow shyly, 'I've already chosen a name for him. I gave him a name at the same time you chose all the others. It seemed wrong for him not to have one ... and I so wanted him not to die.'

Her husband smiled. 'Spill the beans,' he grunted.

'Well,' said the sow, 'I was thinking how heroic this littlest pig would have to be, fighting for life. So I chose a hero's name.' Gazing lovingly at the tiny piglet, she whispered, 'His name is Parsifal.'

The boar was silent for a moment. He had no idea who this 'hero' called Parsifal was. His wife read all sorts of fancy things he couldn't be bothered with. But he didn't want to say so, in case his wife called him pig ignorant. So he dipped one trotter in the parsnip wine and sprinkled the piglet's head, stomach, and each trotter in turn with the wine and then bent down and rubbed the baby's snout with his.

'I name this little pig,' he declared in a voice fit to wake the whole farm, '*Parsifal*.'

The three little pigs remembered and were silent for a while. But it did not do to think for too long about their parents, both of whom had disappeared over a year ago. They dragged their minds back to the present.

'Well, what about this Farmer lark, then?' asked Parsnip, stubbing out his root on a stone.

'Lark? Lark? Did someone call me? Lark? Lark? I'm game for a lark? Chirrup, chirrup, chirree...' sang a lark in the tree above him.

'Oh, not you, you twit!' said Parsnip. 'Buzz off.'

'I can't buzz, but I can fly,' retorted the lark. 'Which is more than you can do, you fat pigs.' She flew away in a huff.

'As I was saying...' Parsnip began.

'Before you were rudely interrupted,' interrupted Parsley.

'Thank you, Parsley,' said Parsnip through gritted teeth. 'Before I was rudely interrupted ... What are we going to do about the Farmer?'

'It does seem a bit much for him to go off for goodness knows how long and leave the farm in the hands of ... well, hired hands. They obviously don't know what they're doing,' complained Parsifal.

'They have no imagination. No creativity. No *savoir faire*,' sighed Parsley. She tended to read the pages from fashionable and arty magazines that found their way to the farm.

'I wonder when he's going to come back,' said Parsifal. 'Perhaps things will improve then.'

Parsnip struck the stone with his trotter. 'Perhaps he's not going to come back!' he declared.

'What?' said the other two little pigs.

'Perhaps,' said Parsnip in a hushed voice as he beckoned the others to come closer, 'perhaps the Farmer...' and here Parsnip's voice sank to a whisper, 'perhaps the Farmer ... doesn't exist!'

The other two little pigs gasped. They sat silent for at least a minute while they took in this astonishing statement. What *would* Parsnip say next! If the Farmer didn't exist, then anything could happen!

2

No Sty-in-the-Sky?

B ut ... but ... but that's outrageous!' stammered Parsifal. 'The Farmer's got to exist!' cried Parsley. 'Otherwise, how would the farm be here ... and how would we be here?'

'The Farmer must be the one who created the farm,' said Parsifal. 'Parsley's right. There's no way we'd be here without him!'

'I wonder,' said Parsnip quietly, almost as if the others weren't there. Parsnip rose and walked a few paces towards the farm. Then he stopped, rose on his hind legs and stretched to his full height. Behind him, the sun was setting in a blaze of light. To his siblings, he seemed bigger than ever as he stood outlined against the sky. The gentle breeze stirred his ears and tail but not the stubborn bristles that were forming around his snout and mouth.

'He's turning into quite a boar!' giggled Parsley.

'Ssshh,' whispered Parsifal, 'he's thinking.'

Parsnip, still on his hind legs, turned round to address them. His voice had a new authority.

'The Farmer does not exist,' he announced as if he were teaching little piglets. 'He is a myth. An invention. Someone, a long time ago, must have made up the idea of a great big Farmer who created the farm and all the animals as a way of explaining why we're all here. And now the hired hands use the threat of the Farmer returning someday to make us keep all their silly rules and regulations.'

'So the Farmer didn't write down all the rules and regulations for us before he left on his journey?' asked Parsley.

'Does that mean...' Parsifal hesitated, 'does that mean we don't have to stick to them anymore? That we can ... do anything we want?'

'I think that seems logical,' replied Parsnip.

His siblings detected a note of superiority in his tone but they were too much in awe at this development to comment. 'Gosh,' they said. A farm with no rules! Why, anything could happen! Delicious visions of freedom began to creep into their heads.

Parsnip looked away once more towards Far Off Farm.

'Anything is possible for a pig who believes in himself. We can do anything. The little pigs have come of age.'

'Wow!' said Parsley, and with an effort she scrambled up onto her hind legs and tottered over to join Parsnip.

'Gosh!' said Parsifal, and tottered after her.

The three stood in silence (partly because two of them were concentrating on keeping their balance). Then Parsnip spoke again. 'In fact,' he said slowly, 'logically there's nothing stopping us from leaving Far Off Farm altogether!'

The other two pigs were so startled that they had to grab onto their older brother, and almost made him lose his balance—Parsnip had secretly practised walking on his hind legs for weeks.

'You really mean that, don't you?' gasped Parsley. She wiggled her ears as if she couldn't believe what she was hearing.

'Yes!' said the wobbling Parsifal. 'I must admit I've been thinking about this for a while. I've been reading up on building houses in a magazine I found in the rubbish dump and I think I know what to do.'

'You mean build a place of our own?' squeaked Parsley.

'Why not?' said Parsnip. He had been thinking along the same lines. 'We could even build three houses. Then we'd each have our own place to hang out in. And we could invite anyone we wanted to come round.'

'You mean ... we could breed with anyone we wanted to,' said Parsley, going red again.

'Of course,' said Parsnip. 'There'd be no more rules and regulations.'

'So we could eat anything we wanted!' cried Parsifal.

'That's right,' said Parsnip.

The little pigs drew a breath as the implications of their new-found freedom began to sink in.

'It all makes sense,' said Parsley. She began to strut away from the other two. (When, they wondered, did their sister learn to walk like that?) 'Let me get this right—if there's no Farmer, then we don't have to keep all the rules and regulations, which means we can do anything we want.'

Then Parsifal spoke. 'Yes but ... does this mean that there's no Perfect Farm either—you know, where all good little pigs are supposed to go when they die? You know, like Mother told us?'

'Ha!' Parsnip snorted. 'That's all part of the same fairy tale, the myth, don't you see? A Perfect Farm where everything's wonderful, where you get fed and brushed all day, and drink as much as you want, and sleep as long as you like, and all the animals stop eating each other and become friends—yuk!' Parsnip's voice had become sing-song and sarcastic. 'Who wants that anyway?'

The others were silent. They had thought the Perfect Farm sounded rather nice.

Parsley suddenly turned back. She had been looking up at the sky and thinking about the Perfect Farm that their mother had told them about when they were piglets. And now she had noticed that the sky was beginning to look ominously dark as the sun disappeared and clouds gathered.

'So...' She paused to cough. 'You mean there's no sty-in-the-sky when you die?'

'Exactly!' said Parsnip. He laughed.

'So you're saying that Mother lied to us?'

'Oh ... er, no.' Parsnip hesitated. 'I think that Mother genuinely believed all that stuff. I don't think she deliberately lied to us. But she'd learned it from her mother, who'd learned it from her mother, and so on. It's a story that's been handed down for generations. No one was lying ... except perhaps the hired hands in the first place.' Parsnip felt more and more liberated as he elaborated these ideas on the spur of the moment—thinking on his trotters, as it were.

'Does that mean ... but what...' Parsifal was so upset that he was having difficulty forming a sentence.

'Come on, spit it out,' said Parsnip.

'What can you expect from a runt?' said Parsley. 'Runt, runt, runt.'

'Runtie, runtie, runtie,' joined in Parsnip. 'Gruntie, gruntie, gruntie!'

'Shut up, shut up, shut up,' cried Parsifal.

'Huh, for the last of the "litter", read "rubbish",' said Parsley.

'Shut your snout!' cried Parsifal. His eyes flashed, his snout quivered and his fat trembled with rage.

'Runtie, gruntie, runtie!' the other two carried on for a while. They laughed so much they almost toppled off their hind legs and had to lean on each other for support.

'Come on, let's get serious,' said Parsnip finally. He wiped his snout on his arm.

'Just remember I'm bigger than both of you now,' Parsifal yelled. He stood in a huff a few yards away with his back to them.

'Yes, fatso,' mumbled Parsley in Parsnip's ear. They both giggled.

'No, seriously,' said Parsnip as he ambled over to Parsifal. 'What vital thing was it you wanted to say to us?'

Well, if you really want to know,' said Parsifal, 'I was wondering ... if there's no sty-in-the-sky-when-you-die—if there's no Perfect Farm that we go to if we've been good little pigs—then what happened to Mother and Father when that van took them away?' He finished in a rush, as if he didn't want to hear himself asking the question.

The other two were silent for a while. They had not considered this. They all remembered that terrible night when they had stood squealing and shrieking while the hired hands trussed up their parents and dragged them out to a waiting van. They hadn't even had a chance to say goodbye. The hired hands had driven off grinning. They knew where the old sow and boar were going even though the little pigs did not.

'I don't know. How am I supposed to know all the answers?' Parsnip cried.

'Funny, you were talking as if you did,' retorted Parsifal.

Parsley had been looking towards the Whispering Wood as her brothers argued. 'Wasn't there something else that Mother taught us? Or was that part of the myth too?' she asked.

'What?' Parsnip's tone was impatient.

'The B.W.,' she whispered. 'You know.'

A sudden growl of thunder shook the very ground under them followed by a flash of lightning. Parsley shrieked and clung to Parsnip. The Whispering Wood came alive in the wind. Its branches shook and reached towards them. As the darkness fell, the wood began to whisper. *'Bi...i...i...g Wo...o...o...lf, Bi...i...i...g Wo...o...o...lf ... Bi...i...i...g Wo...o...o...lf'* it seemed to repeat over and over again in a low voice that made the little pigs go cold from the tops of their ears to the tips of their trotters.

'It ... it ... it's all a myth!' cried Parsnip. He had hoped his voice would sound commanding, but instead it came out cracked and stammering. 'Th...th...there isn't a B...b...b...Big Wolf who eats little p...p...p...pigs! That was all a fairy tale, a n...n...nursery story! I don't believe in it!'

The thunder crashed again and the lightning bathed the menacing branches with a lurid light. It looked as if the trees were lurching towards them. And all the time the whispering went on and on, *'Bi...i...i...g Wo...o...o...lf, Bi...i...i...g Wo...o...o...lf ...'*

Without so much as glancing at one another, the three little pigs dropped to all fours and scuttled back to Far Off Farm as fast as their twelve little legs could carry them.

3

The Great Escape

The storm that night was one of the worst the little
pigs could remember. It was as if the wind was trying
to uproot Far Off Farm and hurl it into the heavens.
After their troubled sleep, mingled with nightmares of the
(sshhh) *B.W.,* the exhausted little pigs prised open their
eyes.

'Ow!' said Parsnip.

'Ouch!' said Parsley.

'Why is it so bright?' said Parsifal. 'I can hardly see.'

The reason soon became clear.

'Look!' Parsnip cried. 'There's no roof!'

The corrugated tin roof over their sty had vanished.
Above them there was now only a glorious blue sky. They
hurried outside, hoping that their trough hadn't been
blown away too. A hot breakfast would go down very well
after such a night. But what a sight met their eyes.

The fences were down, the feeding troughs were
upturned at the side of the shed, and the farm rubbish dump
seemed to cover the ground as far as the eye could see.

It was a pig's paradise.

'Whooppee!' cried Parsnip, diving into the nearest pile of trash.

'Wheee, heee, heee!' screeched Parsley, rolling over and over in the dirt.

'Wow!' said Parsifal as he stood staring at the mess of magazines, bottles, bits of farm machinery and food that had blown into their sty. It was obviously time to start a game.

An hour later, when the three little pigs had finished throwing things at each other and chasing each other around what had been their sty, they dropped down together in exhaustion. For a late brunch they munched on some potatoes and slurped some of the slops that they'd been able to rescue from the troughs. Leaning against each other, they idly flicked through magazines that had blown their way.

'This is the life!' said Parsnip as he admired photos of the most beautiful mansions and most expensive houses in the country.

'I couldn't agree more,' sighed Parsley, as she studied the pages of *Vanity Farm,* with its glossy photographs of sleek animals who had starred in recent movies and had been seen at the best parties. She was particularly impressed with the pig pin-up of the month. 'I wouldn't say no to being his party animal,' she murmured to herself.

Meanwhile Parsifal was drooling over a page of gourmet recipes. This food looked a lot better than hot slops and potato peel. He would like to try all the recipes that called for chocolate, fresh cream, peanuts, toffee or marshmallow— or preferably all of them at once.

He turned the page, expecting more culinary delights. But what he saw turned his face pale beneath the dirt. In large letters at the top of the page was:

PIGS IN PUBERTY!
A Delicious Delicacy
Brought to you by
Our Very Own Gourmet Chef
Gourmet 'Get-em-while-they're-young' Guzzler
(Special contributor to *The Pig Slaughterers' Monthly*)

The recipe that followed involved young pigs (just like them) cooked in a spicy sauce.

The Pig Slaughterers' Monthly!

What was a magazine like this doing on the farm?

He tried to tell Parsnip and Parsley what he had found, though they would not believe him at first. But they could not deny the evidence when he showed them a picture of the body of a young pig lying sprawled on a bed of lettuce and tomato—and parsley! Parsley ran off to be sick. The other two forced themselves to read on, and found that this poor little pig had been cooked on something called a spit.

'I can't believe that they would spit on him as well, the ... the ... humans!' cried Parsnip.

'I wonder if that's what happened to...' began Parsifal, and then stopped. He couldn't say what they were both thinking. They didn't want to know what had happened to their parents. They stood trembling. The only sound came from Parsley, retching into a trough in the background.

'We've got to do something,' said Parsifal quietly.

'I'll show you what we're going to do,' said Parsnip. He seized the magazine with his teeth, shook it and ripped it into a thousand pieces that floated down around him like confetti.

'Now I'll tell you what we're going to do,' said Parsnip.

'What?' asked Parsifal in an awed whisper.

'We're going to escape, that's what,' said Parsnip. He set his jaw and his eyes were bright. He rose slowly onto his hind legs, threw his head back and let out a long unearthly howl that made Parsifal shudder down to his trotters. He had never heard a pig make a noise like that before.

It would be easy to escape. Most of the fencing around the farm had been blown down and the hired hands had not bothered to start mending it yet.

The three little pigs decided to wait till darkness fell. They didn't want the hired hands to unleash their dogs on them as they ran away. So they spent the rest of the day getting ready to leave. They gathered scraps of food for the journey and some magazines for entertainment (though not the *Pig Slaugh...* you know). They smeared themselves with even more dirt than usual for camouflage. Everything seemed to be going well. The only problem was that, as the sky grew darker and the wind began to blow hard again, the little pigs couldn't help conjuring up images of a big bad wolf who might be lurking on the edges of the farm or waiting in the Whispering Wood, ready to pounce on any little pigs who passed.

But they were determined, and perhaps even more afraid of the fate they might meet if they stayed, and so as the pale light of the moon shone over the farm the three little pigs began their Great Escape.

Parsnip, whose face was dirtier than the others, led the way. 'When I give you the signal,' he whispered, 'just run for it as fast as you can. Run and run and run and don't look back!'

And so they did. They crept out of the sty on their stomachs to keep as low a profile as possible. They crept warily past the rubbish dump, past the dog kennels, past the stables, and then ... they ran.

And they ran and they ran and they ran. They ran across a field, past the pond, away from the barn, along a path, and out into *freedom!*

Only Parsley gave a backward glance. Then, with a great gulp, she turned away from the farm.

None of the three little pigs would ever see Far Off Farm again.

4

Pigs Can Have It All

After they had been running for almost an hour, Parsnip stopped. He was puffing and panting (he was a very fat little pig) and could only gasp, 'It's no good ... I can't go any further! Go ... go ... go on without me. There ... there ... there's the beach. That looks like a good place to live. And there's straw in the fields back there. I can ... can ... build my house with that. Bye-bye, suckers!'

His brother and sister gazed after him in dismay as Parsnip turned away and headed for the beach. They could hear the crash of the distant waves and smell the salt in the air. Parsley was tempted to stay there too.

'Oh come on,' Parsifal said, 'We can't stop running this soon.' He started to jog away, and Parsley followed reluctantly.

But it wasn't long before she keeled over, trotters in the air.

'It's no good, I can't go on!' she cried. 'I'll just have to stay here. There are lots of sticks and bits of wood over there. That will have to do. I'll use them to make my new house.'

'You can't give up, just like that!' cried Parsifal.

'I'm not giving up,' said Parsley, struggling onto her trotters again. 'I think the beach is the best place. It will be beautiful. Why don't you stop here with us?'

'Oh no, not me,' said Parsifal. He was horrified. 'You should never build a house on sand! How will you have any foundations? How will it stand up in a storm? Think of the storm last night! How could any house built on sand stand up to that?'

'It will if I give it thick walls,' said Parsley, tossing her head.

'But that's not good enough,' said Parsifal. 'We need to find good solid ground where we can dig deep foundations. And we need to find top-quality building material that can stand up to any storm. I read all about it in the *Brickbuilders' Gazette* that blew into the sty. Straw and sticks just aren't good enough.'

'Well,' Parsley sighed, 'that's your opinion. I like the beach.'

'You've never seen the beach! You're a pig!'

'I have so. I didn't read the travel sections of *Vanity Farm* for nothing. I think it looks ideal. And if it's good enough for Parsnip, then it's good enough for me. It's only because of him that we escaped at all.'

Parsifal glared at her. What was she playing at?

'You do what you want—' he began.

'Oh, thank you very—'

'But I want something that's going to last. I don't want to be shaking down to my trotters every time the wind gets up or the sky looks like a storm's coming. You'll be at the mercy of every strong gust of wind that comes along. If your houses blow down at the first puff, don't blame me.'

'I won't! Goodbye!' yelled Parsley.

She didn't even watch Parsifal as he turned and ran on. It was to be a very long time before he would see his brother and sister again.

Meanwhile, Parsnip was rubbing his trotters in delight at the thought of his new life in the sun and on the sand. He was so glad he'd stopped running. Over the next month, he built himself a fake Victorian mansion made entirely of straw. It was a replica of a house he had seen in the glossy magazine section of *Vanity Farm.* All the animals who passed 'oohed' and 'aahed' when they saw it.

Parsnip also decided that he didn't much care for being a pig. Other animals looked as if they had a lot more fun. And there was one animal in particular that had caught his eye in the pages of the revered magazine. It was a special type of human being called a 'celeb-rit-y'. This strange breed had apparently first appeared on something called 'Big Brother' and needed no talent or skills or even good looks—they just needed to be pursued by some other odd creatures called 'pap-araz-zi'. For some reason, this made them extremely rich. How one could be famous for being famous was a mystery to Parsnip, but he'd taken one look at the description of this animal's habits and lifestyle and thought: 'That's the life for me!' He knew it was his destiny to be a celebrity.

So he furnished his new mansion in accordance with the lifestyle to which he planned to become accustomed. He had designer troughs installed in the spacious kitchen. Over the mantelpiece in the lounge he put a framed sampler that read: 'I SHOP THEREFORE I AM'. He saved up to go on a special vacation for single pigs in the South of France ('Club Shed'), hoping to meet a lady pig in the top slop bracket. He took up gourmet cooking and was soon turning potatoes into *Pommes de Terre aux Pistils de Safran,* turnips into *Gratin de Navets,* and any vegetables he could lay his trotters on into *Petits Légumes au Vinaigre de Miel.* He spent every night attending as many parties as possible.

He knew it was his destiny to be a celebrity

Then he would come home at dawn, collapse into bed, and wake up to do it all over again.

In the midst of all this excitement, Parsnip now and again remembered that there was supposed to be a big bad wolf that stalked the neighbourhood, trying to catch little pigs. He wasn't keen to end up as an ingredient in a gourmet recipe himself, so he preferred to dismiss this idea as just a rumour made up by other animals who were jealous of his social position and wanted to spoil his fun!

But one day, as he was sitting outside enjoying the sunshine and admiring the finishing touch to his house—the brass nameplate that read 'PARSNIP PIG ESQUIRE—CELEBRITY'—a dark shadow fell over him.

Trembling right down to his trotters, Parsnip turned and looked over the top of his shades. And there, right behind him, was a very large WOLF.

He promptly forgot all about the 'power paw-shake' he was supposed to practise with strangers to impress them. Instead, he shot squealing into his house and slammed the door. He tried to squeeze behind one of the designer troughs in the kitchen and shook like a dandelion in the wind as the dark shadow stalked slowly around the straw mansion.

There was an ominous knock at the door, and a big gruff voice said, 'HELLO, LITTLE PIG! I KNOW YOU'RE IN THERE. COME OUT! I HAVE SOMETHING TO SAY TO YOU.'

But Parsnip shouted back, 'Go away, you big bully! Why are you trying to spoil things for me? I was alright till you came along.'

Next thing he knew, the wolf was rattling at the windows. 'COME OUT, LITTLE PIG! I DON'T MEAN YOU ANY HARM.'

'I'm sure!' Parsnip yelled back. 'You're not having me for your dinner. Go away!'

But the wolf did not give up that easily.

'IF YOU WILL NOT COME OUT, AND YOU WILL NOT LET ME IN, I'LL HUFF, AND I'LL PUFF, AND I'LL BLOW YOUR HOUSE DOWN!'

'Oh, please,' thought Parsnip, 'don't lay this macho stuff on me. Who is this philistine, anyway? Has he no respect for privacy and property?'

But then he heard a terrible sound. It was a whistling, followed by a wild blowing, and soon a gale was whipping around his precious house, ripping away piece after piece of it. Within minutes even the designer troughs had disappeared and the poor celebrity pig was left standing alone, with only his designer underwear between him and the big wolf.

He was so stunned by it all he forgot to suck in his stomach.

Meanwhile, what of Parsley? A short distance away on the same beach, Parsley had built herself a pretty little cottage made entirely of sticks. It was a delightful work of art. It was a pity that nobody could see it.

For Parsley had gone to a great deal of effort to build a thick wall to completely surround her cottage. She had heaved as many logs as she could find into place, and had even added a few dead tree trunks. These were stacked together in formation so that the stick cottage was entirely protected. I don't know how she managed all this on her own. She certainly hadn't asked anyone else for help in case they expected her to be grateful to them afterwards. She was determined to be independent in her new life away from the rules and regulations of the farm. Not only would this wall protect her from anyone outside her cottage, it would also stop anyone from seeing what she was getting up to inside.

But after a few months of living unseen and unvisited in her glorious state of independence, Parsley became a very depressed little pig. She wandered around her house sighing, saying 'Ho, hum', and then, 'I might have known', and, 'Well, at least I have my health', followed by a forced little cough.

Now Parsley had not forgotten the story of the big wolf who had a penchant for eating little pigs. Quite the contrary. She was obsessed by the idea of the big wolf and lived in perpetual fear. She became convinced that he was lurking around every corner and behind every tree. Every night before she went to bed she would bolt each door of her cottage ten times, lay out a few patented wolf traps on the carpet under each window, and take one last lingering look at the strong wall from her bedroom window before she dared go to sleep. What a relief it was that she had found the strength to build that wall to keep her perpetually safe from ... well, from everyone and everything. In order to get to sleep she did not count sheep; instead she would mutter, 'My fence is my defence ... My fence is my defence ... My fence is my defence', until she entered a mild state of unconsciousness.

So when the big wolf really did come to her house, Parsley was almost pleased. All her worst fears were confirmed.

'I told you so,' she panted to no one in particular as she ran to stack all the furniture against the door. 'I told you this would happen!'

'COME OUT, LITTLE PIG,' boomed the wolf, leaning over the garden wall (he was very big). 'I HAVE SOMETHING TO SAY TO YOU!'

'You have to be joking! I know you want to eat me alive. Although why you want to bother with a poor dejected little pig like me, I have no idea.'

'THEN LET ME COME INTO YOUR HOUSE WHERE WE CAN TALK!'

'No, no,' squealed Parsley, 'my house is too small for you. And you wouldn't like me anyway, no one does. You frighten meee!'

So the wolf spoke the fatal words. 'IF YOU WILL NOT COME OUT, AND YOU WILL NOT LET ME IN, THEN I'LL HUFF AND I'LL PUFF, AND I'LL BLOW YOUR HOUSE DOWN!'

Now secretly Parsley thought that the walls she had built around her house were so strong that even this huge wolf could not break them down. So she hid behind the sofa with a box of chocolates and a grim little smile on her face, prepared to wait out the siege.

But what was that noise?

There was a creaking. And a cracking. And then a tremendous RRROOOAAARRR as the thick wooden wall around Parsley's cottage gave way, knocking down her wall and her house all in one go!

Parsley managed to scramble out from under the rubble. With several tearful sniffs she stood all alone before the big wolf at last, the one she had feared for so long.

She was feeling very sorry for herself. She was wearing the old dressing gown she hadn't bothered to change out of for days and she still had curlers in her tail. But now it was too late to make something of herself.

'WELL, WELL, WELL, WHAT HAVE WE HERE,' murmured the big wolf as he advanced upon her.

5

On the Rocks

Meanwhile, what of Parsifal?

The third little pig had run on much further—away from Far Off Farm, away from the woods, and away from the beach and the other little pigs. Parsifal was determined that the new house he was going to build would be built right. It was far too important to be left to chance or a whim. His new house would be built on solid ground with deep foundations.

Every so often he would stop running, wipe the sweat from his forehead, and consult the *Brickbuilders' Gazette* that had blown into the sty on the night of the storm. One article made it clear that it was fatal to build your house on sand. A house should be built on rock so that it has something firm to stand on and so that its foundations will not be affected by winds and storms.

Parsifal had been very tempted to stay with his brother and sister and build his house on the sand near them. A sea view would have been lovely. But he gritted his teeth and carried on running. For him, it was the best or nothing.

So when he found his trotters becoming sore from running on what had turned from sand to rough grassland, to grassland mixed with pebbles, and finally to pure grey granite, Parsifal gave a squeal of delight and did a little dance (fortunately no one was there to see him). At last! This would be his home—he could feel it. There were large stones lying around that would be just the right size for bricks. All he had to do was decide which way the house should face for the best view.

It is very difficult for a pig to hold a pickaxe. It kept chafing the skin around his trotters as Parsifal tried to get a good grip. He found that lifting it high above his head and bringing it down with a loud grunt helped it to penetrate a bit further into the resistant rock. But there was no denying that it was hard going, and he began to lose heart.

One night as he lay beneath the stars, trying to find a comfortable sleeping position on his granite bed, he turned to look at his little plot of land. He had marked out the plan of his dream house with small poles and flags stuck at crooked angles into the rock.

The flags fluttered pathetically in the soft breeze and the harsh light of the moon revealed that he had only managed to carve out a few feet of the merciless rock. Parsifal rolled onto his back again and covered his eyes. He couldn't bear to look. A tear trickled down his cheek. There seemed to be no hope.

He brushed the tears away and gazed up at the sky, hoping for inspiration. But the black night sky and the silver stars were silent. They had nothing to say to him. They were too high up to take any notice of a little pig's despair.

'Is there no hope anywhere? No help anywhere?' he mouthed at the moon. 'Can anyone hear me?'

The wind rustled in the distant trees. A lone bird flew silently overhead, a black silhouette.

Parsifal looked down at the rock. He looked at his sore trotters, wrapped awkwardly in bandages.

'You fool,' the bird seemed to say. 'Do you think anybody cares about you and your silly little house? You're just a dreamer, always have been. The hired hands on the farm knew you would come to nothing and they were right. Look at you! Even when things are impossible, you don't give up. Not if you've got some crazy idea in your head. You're worthless and arrogant. Why didn't you stay with the other little pigs on the beach and be content to build with sticks and straw with no foundations? But oh no, not you! You think you know better than everyone else. You want to go your own way. And this is what it's come down to—sore trotters, sore back, and no home! I hope you're pleased with yourself. You may be a little pig, but you're a big failure!'

Parsifal whimpered and covered his eyes again. He didn't have a friend in the world. The few animals that had passed this remote spot and seen his efforts had laughed and walked away. Some had stayed and stared in disbelief for a while ... and then laughed and walked away.

It was no good. He was a failure, and everyone had known it except him. He must be the laughing stock of Far Off Farm by now, for the birds must have told everyone.

Ah, the farm! Never had it appeared so good to the little pig. He had been a fool. On Far Off Farm there had been soft grass, plenty of food, and friends to talk to. Why had he ever wanted to move out? Oh, he could kick himself—if that were physically possible for a pig. He had reached the end of himself.

As the gentle breeze fanned his face and the silver stars looked down, Parsifal's sniffling turned to sighing, and the sighing turned to soft snores. Even if the answer to his problems had been written in large letters in the sky so that even a pig under stress could understand it, Parsifal was far too exhausted to keep watch and see that. Soon his snores took on their usual ear-splitting porcine proportions.

6

A Helping Paw

The next morning Parsifal was hard at work again. As the sun grew hotter and hotter, his throat began to feel like the bottom of a dried-out trough and he began to cough and cough. He decided he should stop for a drink. He leaned on his pickaxe for a moment and wiped the sweat from his eyes.

As he looked towards the river, he was amazed to see what looked like a very big animal looking in his direction. Parsifal squinted against the sun. He couldn't make out exactly what sort of an animal it was, for in the heat haze the figure was blurry and shimmering against the sky. Whatever it was, it was enormous. It was also standing directly in Parsifal's path to the river, where he needed to go to get a drink.

Parsifal groaned. He didn't feel like making small talk with strangers today. And he certainly didn't want anyone else laughing at his plans for a house. Perhaps if he just went on with his work the creature would get bored and go away. So Parsifal sighed, took a deep breath, and heaved his pickaxe into the air again.

But the very big animal obviously didn't get bored easily. Every time Parsifal looked up from his work, it was still there. And each time it was closer ... and closer ... and closer. Parsifal began to feel rather afraid, for each time he looked the animal appeared bigger ... and bigger ... and bigger.

Soon it was standing only a few yards away, and it was MASSIVE.

'NEED ANY HELP?' the big animal asked.

'Did you say ... help?' Parsifal said in astonishment, hardly able to believe his good luck.

Before he knew what was happening, the big animal had taken the pickaxe from his trotters and had started swinging at the rocky ground with tremendous strength. Granite chips were flying everywhere. Parsifal sat down with a bump and watched in awe for at least an hour. The big animal showed no sign of giving up. On and on it went, methodically swinging the pickaxe. It was almost hypnotizing. And all the time it had a smile on its face, as if it were enjoying some secret thought that was giving it all this energy.

By lunchtime all the foundations had been dug. Parsifal was stunned.

'Wow! How do you do that?' he asked the big animal.

'I AM VERY STRONG AND POWERFUL,' said the big animal in a very matter-of-fact (and very loud) voice.

'Yes, I can see that,' laughed Parsifal. 'But don't you get hot in all that fur? And with those big teeth—you're probably used to eating a lot, huh? Perhaps we'd better have lunch.'

Parsifal had grown hungry just watching all that hard work.

'YES, I AM RATHER HUNGRY,' said the big animal with a wide smile. His teeth glinted in the sun.

With the big animal's help, the third little pig's house was finished within the week. Parsifal was delighted. The house was even bigger than he had originally intended since, halfway through the week, he had rather shyly asked the big animal if he would consider moving in with him when it was finished. (It seemed only right to ask, since the big animal had actually built most of it.) So a few rooms had been added to the original design and the roof was a few feet higher since the big animal was, well ... BIG.

Parsifal had known few, if any, happier moments in his life than that first evening sitting in the living room of his new home after supper. The big animal had just cleared away the supper things (he didn't seem averse to menial domestic tasks either), and the two animals were seated on either side of a cosy fire.

So there they were, the picture of contentment. The little pig smiled dreamily and ran a trotter over his taut full belly—aaahhh, life was good. There was only one thing needed to complete the evening. Parsifal took out a small clay pipe he had recently made. The big animal noticed this and coughed noisily. Parsifal tried to ignore it. He was well aware that his new friend did not enjoy his smoking, but he was determined to do it anyway—as a mark of maturity and independence. Why, he hadn't escaped from Far Off Farm with all its repressive rules and regulations for nothing. He was jolly well going to be master in his own house. Just because the big animal had helped him build it, it didn't mean he had the right to dictate what happened in it. (Parsifal had begun to call his friend 'he' rather than 'it'—now that they were on more personal terms.)

As he tapped the bowl of the pipe on the hearth to clear it out, Parsifal knew that the big animal was about to make some critical remark about smoking (usually it was, 'Fires are supposed to smoke, not pigs'). So it seemed a good idea to try to distract him—to make some comment or ask a question that might lead to a fruitful (and distracting) discussion. He might try asking him the question that had come into his mind on occasions—it hadn't really seemed important when they were busy building the house, but it was something that the little pig should know about his friend, just for future reference.

'Er, just for future reference,' began Parsifal, 'I've been wondering—it didn't really seem important when we were building the house—but I was thinking—now that we're living together and my friends will want to know about you—just what sort of an animal are you, if you don't mind me asking?'

'YOU MEAN YOU DON'T KNOW?' smiled the big animal, his enormous teeth glinting in the firelight.

'I'm afraid I'm a very ignorant pig. You see, I never used to read the magazines that the other little pigs read. I only read ones about how to build houses—and ones about food, of course. I never studied the pictures of other animals; I was never really interested. But in case my friends do ask me about my new housemate, I suppose I should really know, er, what you are,' said Parsifal apologetically.

'ARE YOU SURE YOU WANT TO KNOW?'

'Er, yes.'

The big animal paused and looked up at the ceiling, as if unsure of how to describe himself to the little pig. Then he looked down at Parsifal with his many-toothed smile.

'WELL, THE TWO OTHER LITTLE PIGS CALLED ME THE BIG WOLF, HOWEVER...'

But Parsifal did not hear any more. He had fainted.

7

The White Rabbit

A short while later, Parsifal started to come round. He was vaguely aware that someone was holding a cold flannel to his forehead and that the water was trickling down his face. At first the world looked hazy and indistinct through his half-opened eyes, but as he began to focus Parsifal became aware of a huge face between him and the ceiling. The face was furry with long whiskers and massive buck teeth.

'AAAHHH!'

The little pig jumped up, suddenly remembering why he'd fainted in the first place. He ran to the other side of the room and collapsed against the wall—he was still very dizzy. He looked wildly round the room, but there was no other animal in sight—no trace of the big animal. Where on earth had the Big Wolf gone?

The little pig gingerly made his way around the room with his back to the wall. He looked this way and that, making sure he had the whole room in view so he could spot any sudden moves.

Then he saw them. The tips of two large furry ears peeping over the top of the sofa.

Parsifal looked around for something he could use as a weapon. He was standing by the fireplace. He picked up the coal scuttle, the coal shovel and the poker. He put the scuttle on his head like a helmet. He held the shovel in front of him like a shield. He held the poker like a sword. Thus armoured, he approached the sofa, trying to ignore the coal dust tickling his nose and making him want to sneeze.

The big ears twitched slightly. Parsifal's nose twitched a lot.

Just as Parsifal was preparing to lean over the sofa and inflict the fatal blow, he sneezed. The helmet fell over his eyes, he tripped over the coal shovel and fell heavily on the sofa, nearly impaling himself on the poker. Winded and coughing, Parsifal would not give up. He wrenched off the coal scuttle helmet and launched himself over the back of the sofa. He flailed around with the poker, yelling, 'Take that, and that, and that!'

But the poker hit nothing but air. The Big Wolf had vanished.

Then Parsifal heard a noise behind him and spun round.

A large white rabbit was standing at the other end of the room with its back to the wall, grooming its fur. Parsifal stared. The rabbit stared back. Then it twitched its pink nose in a friendly manner.

It was the whitest, cleanest, furriest, and cuddliest white rabbit that Parsifal had ever seen (and he had seen a lot of rabbits). It was also the largest. It seemed to be regarding him with interest. But what was it doing in his living room? And, more to the point, where was the Big Wolf?

'Who ... who are you?' Parsifal stammered, trying to sound menacing. But the rabbit looked so friendly and endearing that the little pig had to fight the desire to stroke its beautiful fur.

'You can stroke me if you like,' said the rabbit. Its voice was soft and melodious. It was as if it could read Parsifal's thoughts. Its fur looked so soft and strokeable that Parsifal could not resist. He inched over to where the rabbit was standing, feeling like a fool, and put out a tentative trotter to touch that beautiful fur. As he did so, tiny shafts of rainbow-coloured light began to leap off the rabbit's fur and shoot around the room like starbursts. The little pig felt suddenly, ecstatically happy—as if he would burst with joy and satisfaction. He buried his snout in the pure soft fur. The rabbit stroked the top of Parsifal's head and said soothingly, 'There, there, you've had a dreadful shock. You need to rest. Perhaps we should sit down on the sofa.'

Parsifal allowed himself to be led over to the sofa. He didn't care what happened as long as he could cling to that wonderful fur. He felt life and love flowing into him and he became drowsy with sleep and happiness. Who cared where the Big Wolf was now? Parsifal had ceased to be afraid. Who could be afraid of a white rabbit—even a very large one?

'I think I need to explain a few things to you,' said the large white rabbit. 'Close your eyes.'

Parsifal smiled dreamily and did as he was told. He felt the rabbit move away from him, and heard some strange creaking and rustling and grunting noises. What was going on?

'Can I open my eyes yet?' he asked.

There was a silence followed by some more rustling and grunting. 'Aaalright, yooouuu can ooopen them nooowww,' said a voice that didn't sound like the large white rabbit's anymore. It was deep and rich and mellow, and it sounded very familiar to the little pig.

Parsifal warily opened his eyes.

8

The Holy Cow

There before him stood a huge mid-brown milk cow. She had large brown eyes that looked infinitely kind, bright shining hooves, and a majestic swishing tail. Her face bore some resemblance to the large white rabbit's, although it was hard to say exactly how. Perhaps it was something about her strong and loving smile, her fragrant breath, her air of confidence and authority. Parsifal rubbed his eyes in astonishment.

'Where has the big rabbit gone?' Parsifal demanded. 'And who are you?'

'Whooo am I?' the big cow lowed. 'Why, I am the big rabbit.'

She nodded her head and the golden bell around her neck tinkled. She looked majestic—a Queen of Cows, a Holy Cow.

'You can't fool me!' Parsifal exploded. 'I didn't live on a farm for nothing. I think I know the difference between a rabbit and a cow!'

Parsifal may have sounded tough, but he didn't feel tough inside. He didn't want to be rude to the Holy Cow—

partly because she was much bigger than he was, but also because she was the most awe-inspiring cow he had ever seen. There was an aura of peace and contentment around her that Parsifal wished he felt inside him. But all he felt was confusion.

'I tooold yoouu I would explain, if yooouu can be a patient little pig,' mooed the Holy Cow.

Parsifal found himself sitting up straight with his trotters folded over his stomach, waiting with lowered eyes in perfect patience.

'There is much you do not knooow, little pig,' lowed the Holy Cow, 'much that I have come here to tell yoooouu. When I say that I am the Big Rabbit, I am not lying to you, for indeed all rabbits everywhere worship me as their God and were created through me. I am the Ultimate Rabbit, the Big Rabbit.'

The Cow drew herself up to her full height and continued in her soothing, gentle, but authoritative voice:

'Indeed I am also the Great Cow, the Holy Cow, worshipped by all cows everywhere, for they draw their being from me and were created in my image.'

Parsifal looked up. He hardly dared anticipate what the Great Cow, er, Big Rabbit, would say next. The Great Cow seemed to read his thoughts as the Big Rabbit had done.

'Yoooou are wondering what happened to the Big Wolf, of whooom you were sooo afraid. I will explain.'

Parsifal took a deep breath and waited. He hardly dared hope.

As the last rays of the sun flickered through the window, the Great Cow continued.

'I only seem to be the Big Wolf to those who fear me, whooo see me as an enemy come to destroy what they hold dear. I do not seek to destroy my creatures—only those things that would keep them away from me.'

The Holy Cow shook her head sadly.

'Yooou little pigs have been sooo badly taught. The hired hands who were supposed to look after you on Far Off Farm did not do their job well. You were brought up to be afraid of me rather than viewing me as your friend. Just because I'm big doesn't mean I'm bad!'

'I can see now that you're not bad,' said Parsifal quietly.

'Good, good. My creatures only see me that way when they don't really knooow me. They know that I am big and so they are afraid of me, afraid of what I will dooo to them. Silly primitive fear! They try to hide away from me in houses they build for themselves—silly feeble houses made of straw and sticks' (Parsifal blushed for his brother and sister) 'not good solid houses made of brick and, most importantly, made with my help. But twooo can play at that game. If my dear creatures insist on building thick walls to keep me out of their lives, I will come and huff and puff and blooow them dooowwwn!'

'Gosh!' said Parsifal after a fitting pause.

He thought of a question he would like to ask. But would it be impertinent? He was desperate to find out everything now.

'Er, your Majesty, Holy Cow, I was wondering...' the little pig began.

'Yeees?'

'If you're not the Big Wolf, then how do you appear to wolves? I mean, if you're their God too, and they're made in your image, and all that?'

The Great Cow lowed a musical laugh. 'What a clever little pig! I will answer you. Of course I can appear to wolves as a wolf—I can do anything. I am omnipotent! (That's 'all-powerful' to you!) But I am the Big Good Wolf—not the Big Bad Wolf! And not many wolves bother to seek me at all, I'm afraid. They have forgotten how to be good. They were the ones who put around the ugly rumour that the Big Animal is as nasty as they are. They wanted to frighten you other animals and to bend you to their will. They will be punished for this. They have given me some very bad publicity!'

'Wow!' said Parsifal. He was glad he wasn't one of the wolves that had annoyed this Big Almighty Animal.

But the Great Cow was shaking away a tear that had welled up in her eye as she had been talking about her poor deluded creatures.

'It amazes me,' she murmured, half to herself, 'the things my creatures will do to avoid being loved by me.' As she shook her massive head, another tear fell to the ground. It shone with all the colours of the rainbow. The little pig almost expected to see flowers spring up where it had fallen.

'If you will excuse me for saying this,' Parsifal said timidly (for he now knew that this was a Very Important Animal indeed), 'I think that some of your creatures choose to be afraid of you because they don't want someone who's bigger than they are telling them what to do. I know my brother and sister and I used to hate it on the farm when the hired hands told us what to do. They loaded us down with lots of silly rules and regulations. They expected *us* to be really good all the time, but we knew *they* weren't. They certainly didn't keep the rules themselves. And we thought that you—er, I mean the Big Wolf—was just something they'd made up to make us obey them.'

The Great Cow nodded. 'And to sooome extent you were right,' she lowed. 'The hired hands were not all they should have been and did abuse my name to manipulate my creatures. They, too, will have to face me one day to explain their actions.'

'Hmm.' Parsifal pondered this.

'But you,' she said softly, 'have done the right thing. You built your house on the rock with deep foundations and you let me help you and live with you. You are a very blessed little pig.'

'Oh, gosh, thank you!' Parsifal glowed with pleasure. 'But...' Another question had occurred to him. Dare he ask another?

'Ask away,' said the Great Cow.

'Well...' Parsifal hesitated. How should he put it? 'Seeing as you're not the Big Bad Wolf ...'

'Mooowst definitely not!'

'Does that mean you are really a Rabbit or a Cow? Or aren't you like any of us? I mean, I still don't know what you really are.'

The Great Cow laughed again. Parsifal went red. He must have said something stupid.

'I am neither a Rabbit nor a Cow,' announced the Holy Cow. 'I am merely showing myself to you in a form you can understand—one that won't frighten you. Yoooou cannot see me as I really am, you know. Not in this life.'

'Oh.' Parsifal was disappointed. He had hoped he would understand more than this. 'But if you aren't a Rabbit or a Cow, I ... I ... don't know how to think of you. I need to think of you as Something. Are you normally invisible?'

'Nooormally,' said the Cow in a matter-of-fact voice. 'But I can see you need more help. I think there is something more I can do. This will be one of the greatest lessons you will ever learn. You must never forget it as long as you live,' said the Great Cow. 'Close your eyes!'

Parsifal did as he was told, and covered his eyes with his trotters for good measure. But the temptation was too great. Without really meaning to, he found his eyes opening just a slit so that he could see the Big Animal through the gap in each trotter.

Something very strange was happening. The Big Animal was changing shape before his eyes.

He heard some popping, grunting, and thwacking sounds. The tail grew shorter and curlier, the face longer and snoutier, and the body shorter and stumpier until, towering in front of him, dominating the whole room, was the Big Pig himself!

His body was sleek and the perfection of fat, his nostrils were enormous, his ears rested at perfect angles to his head, and his eyes had the same merry loving smile that had delighted Parsifal in the Large White Rabbit and the Holy Cow. Here, indeed, was the one and only perfect Pig, the essence of pighood.

Parsifal threw himself down at the Big Pig's trotters in worship. 'My Lord and my God!' he gasped.

The Big Pig laid a huge trotter on the little pig's head and blessed him, saying, 'Now you know, now you understand. Now you are seeing me more clearly. I created you and you have your being through me. I willed that you exist, my dear little pig. You belong to me. Never forget this. And whatever happens in the future, remember that I love you and never let that go. That knowledge will sustain you through many a trial, for trials will come. For you are a chosen pig—not for destruction, but for life, for the life that I will give you.'

The Big Pig waved his other trotter in an arc that created the after-image of a rainbow around the room.

'This is a good house,' the Big Pig pronounced. 'Live in it—be happy and healthy and get fit for the tasks ahead, for, yes, I do have work for you to do.'

Work? Parsifal's heart sank a bit. Work? What could the Big Pig mean? And what was this talk about getting fit? He looked down at the six spare tyres that showed around his

The Big Pig laid a huge trotter on the little pig's head and blessed him

waist as he leaned forward. Perhaps he should ask the Big Pig another question to distract him from all this talk about work and fitness.

'Er, Big Pig, your Majesty, there's just one more thing.'

'Yes?'

'I still don't know what you look like really—when you're alone. I understand that you're not one animal more than any other and that you're greater than any of your creatures, but...'

'Come over here and sit down,' laughed the Big Pig. 'I can see this is going to be a long night.' He squeezed himself into one of the larger armchairs and waited until Parsifal sat down at his trotters on the floor. The Big Pig stroked his head and asked, 'Do you know what an incarnation is?'

Parsifal thought for a while. 'It's a sort of flower, isn't it?' he said hopefully.

'Never mind,' laughed the Big Pig.

'Oh, and another thing,' said Parsifal, 'if you appear to me as the Big Pig, so I can really understand you and get to know you better, then what about human beings—like the hired hands? Have you ever appeared to them in human form? I don't think I'd dare, if I were you. Those humans can be pretty nasty. I dread to think what they would try to do to you. They're more vicious than any animals I know.'

The Big Pig stopped stroking Parsifal's head and sighed with great sadness. Parsifal looked up in confusion. Was it something he had said? Were those tears in the Big Animal's eyes again? Oh dear, I must have put my trotter in it again, thought Parsifal. Open mouth, insert trotter—that's what Parsley always used to say about me. Oh dear.

But the Big Pig smiled down at him. 'You ask some very interesting questions, little pig,' he said. 'But for the time being there is just one thing you need to know.' The Big Pig's voice was a whisper as he bent down to snuffle into the little pig's ear: 'Remember you are loved. That's all you need to know. For now.'

'Mmm.' Parsifal found himself becoming sleepy as the Big Pig began to stroke his head again. 'But...'

'Ssshhh. Remember the Perfect Farm in the sky where good little pigs go when they die?'

'Mmm...'

'Remember that the Great Farmer lives there, the One who made everything there is?'

'Mmm...'

'Well here is another great mystery for you to dream about tonight.' The Big Pig's voice sank to a whisper again. 'I and the Farmer are One,' he said.

But Parsifal's snores drowned out this astounding statement. It had all been too much.

The Big Pig laughed quietly and took the little pig up in his arms. It was time for bed. He carried Parsifal up the stairs and tucked him under the blankets. He gave Parsifal one last loving look—a pig he knew inside out and still loved.

Then the Big Animal disappeared.

There was work to do elsewhere that night.

(a few years later ...)

9

Health Hazards for Pigs

I t was spring again. Birds were chirping, lambs were cavorting, and rabbits were rampant. Even Parsifal Pig could not deny that another season was indeed rolling round, with all that meant for a pig who had spent most of the winter either snuggled in a warm bed or with his snout in a trough of hot swill. The resulting rolls of fat meant that his arms were somewhat further away from his sides than they used to be.

How had this happened? How had Parsifal, who had been such a good little pig, and was getting to know the Big Animal so well, managed to get into this state?

In a word ... FOOD.

Food had been Parsifal's undoing—and not just any food, but the sort of luscious, delicious, oozing, schmoozing, lip-licking, luxury food found only in gourmet magazines. Just one look at a chocolate marshmallow and cream anything, and Parsifal was a goner. The Big Animal had warned Parsifal that this was not good food for pigs, and he kept talking about the fact that Parsifal should mix with other pigs and get healthy and fit and do some *work* (the other four-letter word responsible for the little pig's downfall—because of his avoidance of it). But Parsifal would mutter something (through a mouthful of his latest Chocoholic's White Chocolate Truffle Green Marzipan Surprise) about work being something for tomorrow, not today, and carry on troughing. Even when the Big Animal started speaking very sternly about his going on a detoxification programme to be purified of his indulgence in the flesh, Parsifal took no notice. The truth is, he could hardly hear the Big Animal at all now over his snaffling and snuffling at heaps of food and drink and the mighty sonic snores that followed.

Over a period of a year, the Big Animal's visits became less and less frequent. But Parsifal hardly noticed. Even though the Big Animal had been very nice, and impressive, Parsifal had silently decided that he didn't want anyone telling him what to do after all. He might as well have stayed on Far Off Farm to be oppressed by all the silly rules and regulations there. His brother and sister had been right. It had been good to escape all that and branch out on one's own. Even if the Big Animal had created him, surely that didn't mean that a pig had to kow-tow to the Big Animal for the rest of its life? What about having a bit of fun now and again? Surely a bit of self-indulgence here and there wasn't a bad thing? Parsifal just wanted to be independent.

But the 'bit of self-indulgence' had grown from the occasional nibble of a biscuit, to biting into a medium-sized slice of a cake, to a dive into a heaving trough of forbidden fodder. Parsifal slept off each bout of indulgence in an increasingly rank and dirty bed.

And so the Big Animal became invisible to the little pig. Now and again Parsifal felt a sort-of kind presence just behind his shoulder, or seated in the big chair at the other end of the room where the Big Animal used to sit. But Parsifal had begun to shrug off even this. Because to acknowledge the Big Animal's presence would mean that he would have to repent of his bad ways and *change*—and he was not prepared to do that. Not just yet anyway. 'Wait until after you've tried just a little bit of that new Lemon Chocolate Orange Coffee Meringue Nest Cheesecake that's in the fridge waiting for you', a voice inside him seemed to say. The choice between a potentially challenging talk with the Big Animal and a mouth-melting cheesecake provided no contest. The cheesecake won every time.

The few friends that Parsifal had left had begun to bring tape-measures when they visited instead of cake. One or two of them had left magazines on the coffee table for Parsifal to read. They contained articles like 'Health Hazards for Pigs' or 'If You Get Too Fat Your Friends Won't Want to Be Seen with You'. But Parsifal would throw the magazines across the room and head for the fridge.

Soon his friends stopped visiting. Parsifal told himself he didn't care and ate another truffle.

Then one day there was a knock at the door.

Parsifal heaved himself onto his side (he had been lying on his back in the fireplace with his legs in the air) and slowly and painfully rolled over to the door. Who on earth could be inconsiderate enough to call on him after a major food binge? (Following that logic, no one could ever visit him at any time of day or night.) He just about managed to stand upright enough to open the door and peer out, blinking ferociously in the unaccustomed sunshine.

'Who is it?' he said through gritted teeth.

But there was nobody there. He thought he heard giggling—high-pitched giggling, the sort of giggling a baby badger or weasel would indulge in when they were teasing someone. Parsifal stuck his snout suspiciously around the sides of the door. He still couldn't see anyone.

But what was that? There were red blotches of what looked like blood on the garden path. Was someone hurt? Parsifal tottered out unsteadily on his trotters. When he reached the end of the porch he was completely out of breath (it was all of four paces). He looked around. No, there was no one there, nothing to see.

He breathed a sigh of relief, and burped. Gosh, he thought, it must be almost time for elevenses. His stomach was getting a bit restless. Better not keep it unoccupied for long, he thought, who knows what might happen. He turned round to go back to the house.

But in front of him was a terrible sight—his nameplate had been defaced with red paint. Someone had crossed out the 'LITTLE' in front of his name and painted 'HA HA' over it. And instead of 'PARSIFAL' his name now read 'PORKY'.

Our not-so-little pig stormed back into the house and slammed the door, shaking all the blossoms from the trees in the garden as he did so.

Parsifal was shaking, too, as he eased himself into position in front of the grimy mirror in his bedroom. As he studied the vague but enormous form that greeted him, Parsifal made a resolution. It was spring. That meant it would soon be summer. He solemnly swore that he was going to be the slimmest pig on the beach this summer—if it killed him.

He sucked in his stomach and cocked his head at just the right angle so he had only one chin left. His reflection did the same. It was a good start.

Now *how* could he get fit and lose weight? That was the question. Parsifal remembered reading that walking was good for you. Well walking, especially with four legs, sounded easy enough—even he could do that.

So, the next morning (after a good night's hog-snoring and a lie-in for good luck), he stood on the front porch with map and compass in trotter, sunglasses, hat—and a backpack full of food. He took a deep breath and was overtaken by a violent attack of coughing. Oh dear, he thought. Obviously his, er, 'cardboard-vacuum' system, or whatever it was called, needed improvement. His lungs and heart felt as if they were going to burst. Parsifal had heard about this 'cardboard-vacuum' system on a DVD by Jane Gerbil in her 'Low-impact Aerobics for Fat Pigs Who Can't Handle Any More' series (which had also been left on Parsifal's coffee table by a concerned friend). Jane Gerbil was a muscular little animal that Parsifal had begun to have nightmares about. Every time he went to the fridge he could hear her voice warning him with evangelistic zeal to make no allowances for the flesh.

But as Parsifal stood there on the porch he had a nagging feeling that there was something he'd forgotten, and it wasn't the tin opener. No, there was something else, very important, that he'd forgotten. Then he remembered what it was. He lumbered back upstairs and into his bedroom. He stopped in front of a photograph in a silver frame.

It was the only really precious thing he possessed. When he blew off the dust, he could see the picture of his old friend, the Big Animal, in the form of the Big Pig. Oh, how kind the Big Pig had been to him. He had helped Parsifal to build this house after the escape from Far Off Farm. It seemed so long since Parsifal had actually seen the Big Pig.

Parsifal looked round the room. What a mess. There was stuff everywhere and nothing was where it was supposed to be. No wonder the Big Animal didn't turn up much anymore. Parsifal's slovenly habits must have become too much to take. He shed a little tear and snuffled a bit as he remembered his great friend. All the Big Animal had left behind was a note taped to the frame of the photograph with 'Do Not Open' written on the outside. Parsifal had thought it rather strange that the Big Animal had left a note that he wasn't supposed to open, but he hadn't given the matter much thought over the past year or so.

But now, as he wiped the dust from the photograph, the envelope did not read 'Do Not Open!' but 'Open!' (The change was due to a splodge of Peanutbuttermarshmallowfluffchocolatecream Surprise that had inadvertently been flung at the picture during a past food orgy and had now eaten its way through a large section of the envelope.) The pig grimaced as he wondered what that particular culinary delight must have done to the lining of his stomach, but he let it pass. Surely this must be a sign. Strange coincidences often happened when the Big Pig was around, so perhaps his influence was still lingering in the house after all.

Parsifal eagerly ripped open what was left of the envelope and unfolded a sheet of paper. There were a few words on it. It had a weird word at the top that he did not recognize. It said:

FOR YOUR P-I-L-G-R-I-M-A-G-E.

Pil-grim-age? Parsifal had no idea what that meant. He saw that you could make the word 'pig' out of it quite easily, and he spent a few moments puzzling over what other words could be made from the rest of the letters, but he soon gave up. Perhaps the meaning of the word would come to him on his walk when he had more time to think.

The rest of the message was pretty mysterious, too. In the Big Pig's trotter-writing were the words:

REMEMBER YOU ARE LOVED.
P.S. THAT'S ALL YOU NEED TO KNOW
(FOR NOW).

What a strange message, Parsifal thought. And he wasn't supposed to have opened this all those years? Yet the words seemed familiar and, for some reason, they gave Parsifal a warm glow deep inside and conjured up many pleasant memories of the Big Pig's companionship. So Parsifal decided to take the note with him on his walk. He could take it out and read it every so often to cheer himself up.

All he had to do now was find out what this 'pil-grim-age' thing was.

10

The Pil-Grim-Age Thing

A few hours into his walk, the not-so-little pig's trotters were sore, his stomach was growling at passing dogs who were giving him strange looks, and he was convinced that he must have sweated off at least twenty pounds. Instead of glorying in the wonders of creation, he was yearning for his next meal. The river reminded him of lemonade, the trees appeared to be blossoming with his favourite sweets, the flowers all looked like cheese sandwiches on stalks, and the birds were singing the delights of Peanutbuttermarshmallowfluffchocolatecream Surprise.

With a sigh, Parsifal gave in to the pressure and eased himself down under the nearest tree, took out ample amounts of food from his backpack, opened a novel, and ate to his stomach's and heart's content. The more food he ate now, the lighter his backpack would be, and the further he could walk to lose more weight. He should eat as much as possible, he reasoned.

As the sun began to set, Parsifal became sleepier and sleepier, his arms resting on the familiar full stomach. The book of horror stories he had been reading fell out of his trotters. Parsifal fell into a deep sleep.

This was a mistake. No little (or not-so-little) pig should ever fall asleep on a full stomach after reading horror stories in the middle of nowhere. Parsifal had a nightmare.

He dreamt he was being pummelled by a large white rabbit (not *the* White Rabbit) in a black waistcoat with a watch in its paw. The rabbit was yelling in his ear: 'YOU'RE LATE! YOU'RE LATE! FOR A VERY IMPORTANT DATE!'

In the dream, the not-so-little pig woke with a start to see the rabbit haring off down the road, still shouting to the pig: 'YOU'RE LATE FOR THE RACE! YOU'RE LATE FOR THE RACE! AND YOU'RE IN NO SHAPE! YOU'RE IN NO SHAPE!'

Before he knew what was happening, the not-so-little pig found himself in the middle of a large crowd at the starting line of a marathon. An entry form was thrust into his trotter:

ARE YOU FIT FOR THE PERFECT FARM?
RUN THE MARATHON OF LIFE
AND TEST YOUR STAMINA!
P.S. Only Nursery Rhyme and Children's Story Characters Need Apply.

And, indeed, there they all were—stretching as far as the eye could see. There was Humpty Dumpty—looking very dumpy and bad-tempered and far too hot in his clothes already. Next to him were Jack and Jill, who were trying to get themselves patched up in time for the race. But they had started arguing and were throwing the vinegar and brown paper at each other instead. A bit further on stood

Tweedledum and Tweedledee, both glumly looking at their paunches as if they had a joint premonition that they didn't stand a chance.

Just as Parsifal was thinking that perhaps he wasn't too bad compared to the competition, he saw with horror that Jane Gerbil was heading for him. She was coming to judge his fitness to take part in the marathon. With a mere wave at his paunch she dismissed him from the race and pronounced those fatal words: 'TO THE HEALTH FARM WITH HIM!'

As he was being dragged away, Parsifal couldn't help thinking that it sounded more like 'OFF WITH HIS HEAD!'

II

The Health Farm

As Parsifal's dream continued, he was marched by
soldiers made of playing cards for what seemed like
miles and miles. It was as bad as, or worse than,
having to do the marathon. They marched up hills and
down into valleys and up hills again until, in the distance,
at the top of the highest hill of all, appeared a pink neon
sign: 'HEALTH FARM'. Parsifal could just make out the
smaller letters in green below the sign: 'Enter Only if You
Want To CHANGE!'

Our not-so-little pig whimpered. He wasn't sure that he
wanted to change. But he didn't seem to have much choice
at that moment.

As they drew closer and the hill became steeper and
steeper, the health farm seemed to grow bigger and
bigger. Soon it was all he could see—the enormous open
doorway and the huge crowd of animals and nursery rhyme
characters who were also being marched in or who were
walking towards it of their own accord. He even recognized

some of his old neighbours from Far Off Farm, but it hardly seemed appropriate to wave to them.

Soon Parsifal was waiting in the long queue to enter the health farm. He had no idea how long he waited—he tasted that strange combination of eternity and the suspension of time-as-we-know-it that everyone experiences in a very long queue.

But at last he found himself at the front of the line, face to face with a rather cynical-looking cat dressed in pink spandex and a luminous headband. She was enthroned behind a large desk and was filling out the forms for each animal as they went in or were turned away.

Parsifal tended not to like cats.

Cats tended not to like him.

'I think I had better waaarn you before we begin,' began the cat, 'that only those who know they are unfit for the Purrrfect Farm are allowed to enter here. Just so you don't get uppity.'

'Oh, I know I'm unfit,' said the not-so-little pig.

'Then aaall you need to do is recite your catechism, then you may enter.'

'My what?' asked the pig, mystified.

The cat looked impatient. 'I am a cat, so this is a catechism! I should have thought it was obvious! Any more questions?'

'Oh no, no,' muttered the pig, wondering what on earth she was talking about. But since he had come so far, he decided he should go the whole hog and try to get into this place.

The cat stood on her desk, cleared her throat, gave a menacing look at some mice further down the line who were squeaking stupidly, and began to read out the great questions. The pig found himself responding as follows:

Q: What are you by nature?

A: *I am a slob.*

Q: How did you get that way?

I am a slob

A: By catering to the flesh.

Q: Have you any excuses?

A: (hesitating) No.

Q: Then why should we allow you into our health farm when you have no means of payment and cannot justify your actions?

Parsifal was dumbfounded. The cat was right! There was no reason on earth why he should be allowed to get fit for the Perfect Farm. He had nothing to say in his defence. He was in the Trough of Despond. Then he remembered. In his backpack was the note from the Big Pig. He fumbled for the note while the cat rolled her eyes and tapped her paw on the desk. To his relief, the note was still there. As he handed the scruffy bit of paper to the Catechism Cat she gave him the look of disgust of which only cats are capable. He ignored the look. This was his last hope.

Parsifal summoned up all his courage. 'I'm here because ... because ... the Big Animal loves me!' he said.

'OK. You're in,' said the cat.

12

Pilgrim Pig and the Dream Cycle

arsifal was led into the next room, where he was scrubbed and showered. It was good to feel clean again after his long journey. He was then dried off and given a T-shirt to put on (although it took a while to find one big enough). 'IN TRAINING FOR THE LIFE TO COME!' was splashed across the front in big trendy letters. He was also given two pairs of sweat bands, a head band, and an identity badge that read 'Parsifal—Pilgrim Pig'. Parsifal grinned as he pinned this onto his T-shirt in front of a large mirror. (What he didn't notice was that his reflection seemed to scowl back at him slightly.) Another svelte cat took a photograph of him that would be pasted on his locker. A new photograph would be taken every month to provide an encouraging, but more likely embarrassing, 'before-and-after' contrast.

And so Parsifal began a daily regimen of exercise—using the health farm's specialized equipment—and diet—eating lots of fresh fruit and vegetables. Soon his stomach was taut and his biceps were bulging. He felt like a new pig, as though he had been allowed to start life all over again. When he found an exercise hard or the weights heavy, he would repeated 'I am loved, I am loved, I am *loved'* over and over again until he really believed it. And then he would find strength that he hadn't realized he had. He began to teach this technique to the other animals too, as it seemed only fair to remind them that they were also loved. And so Parsifal began to make new friends and end his not-so-splendid isolation.

The days were going quite well. The nights were a different matter.

Parsifal began to have strange dreams (or 'double-dreams', since he was already dreaming?).

The piece of exercise equipment on the health farm that Parsifal particularly liked was a stationary exercise bike called the Dream Cycle. If you used it often enough, it would give you the physique of your dreams. Parsifal began to use this cycle last thing at night before going to bed. He found that the gentle rhythm helped him to unwind after a hard day and got him into the right state of mind to fall asleep as soon as his head hit the pillow (or the rolled-up sports towel he now used instead of a pillow). But one night, the Dream Cycle began to have an odd effect on him. Instead of dreaming that he was tunnelling his way through a mountain of Peanutbuttermarshmallowfluffdoublechocolatecream Surprise as he had always done, his dreams became quite different. And so Parsifal dreamed a dream—a double-dream.

13

Prodigal Pig

In this double-dream Parsifal dreamed that he was a little pig again back at Far Off Farm. He was a very little pig, and his parents were there. He could see them at the other end of the sty and he ran towards them with a squeal of delight. He winded himself as he ran into the granite bulk of his father's body.

'Whoooaa there, Little Pig!' cried his father. 'What are you trying to do? Have you finished your chores yet today?'

As Parsifal turned to hug his mother, his mind was racing. What chores? His parents must have given him some chores to do but he couldn't remember what they were, which probably meant they hadn't been done—not by Parsifal, at any rate.

But if he said 'What chores?' that would be a real giveaway. Then again, if he pretended to have done them when they obviously hadn't been done then he was in trouble again. So all he could say was, 'Erm...'

'Parsifal,' his father said, 'have you been daydreaming instead of working?'

(Parsifal could, of course, have answered, 'I'm not daydreaming, I'm double-dreaming.' But when you're double-dreaming you don't know that you're double-dreaming, so he didn't have an answer.)

'Erm...' said Parsifal again.

'I recognize that "Erm",' said his mother. 'It means he has and he hasn't—he *has* been daydreaming and he *hasn't* done his chores!'

Parsifal knew he was in trouble, and especially when he found out that his siblings had finished their chores hours ago and had been allowed out to play. 'How dare they show me up—the swine!' thought Parsifal.

'Are you rebelling against our authority?' asked his father. 'Are you revolting?'

'No, no, honest I'm not,' he protested.

'Honest-ly, Parsifal,' said his mother, 'the word is honest-*ly*.'

So Parsifal tried to busy himself around the sty doing what he thought his parents might want him to do. But the temptation to fool around and daydream was just too great. Fifteen minutes later, Parsifal was leaning over the fence and gazing into the distance, dreaming what it would be like to leave the farm and go off on his own somewhere. He thought about all the exciting adventures he could have out there where his parents wouldn't be nagging him all the time. It sometimes seemed that anything Parsifal wanted to do, his parents told him not to do. And anything he didn't want to do, his parents wanted him to do. There was no pleasing them.

'So why don't you just run away?' a voice inside him seemed to say. But where would he go? What would he do? How could a very little pig look after himself?

'Isn't there a small stash of money and food hidden at the back of the shed, near where your parents sleep at night?' the same voice seemed to whisper. 'Why don't you take that? Then you could escape and be free of all their "do's" and "don'ts". Don't be a boring boar like your father—go wild!'

It was an appealing idea.

So Parsifal hid behind the shed until nightfall. He didn't reply when he heard his parents shouting for him. Instead he hunkered down to wait until he heard their loud snores from inside the shed.

It took longer than usual for his parents to fall asleep. They seemed to be muttering quite a lot to each other. 'No doubt they're complaining about me again,' thought Parsifal. Finally he heard the snores and knew it was safe to sneak into the shed.

And because this was a dream, a double-dream, Parsifal had no problem extracting the large cache of gold rings from under his father's nose and removing the silk purse from under his mother's ear. He put the gold rings in the silk purse and headed off to begin his adventure.

And because this was a dream, a double-dream, it was only a matter of a moment or two before he found himself walking the streets of a big town. He stared, amazed, into shop windows full of his favourite food (anything made of peanut butter, marshmallow, fresh cream, etc.). And there were flashy clothes to buy that would guarantee him instant friends.

Parsifal threw an enormous party. And another. And another.

Soon he was the most popular pig in town. Everyone laughed at his jokes and his picture was in all the newspapers and glossy magazines. At last he was being recognized for who he really was—the ultimate party animal. Instead of going to bed at sundown, he partied till dawn and slept all day. He could do anything he wanted and there were no parents to say otherwise.

He did wonder now and again what his parents would do about the missing gold rings and silk purse, but when nothing seemed to happen, he stopped worrying. His parents could manage just fine without the nest egg they'd put aside for their old age. They had everything they could want on the farm. The gold and silk was to be passed on to Parsifal and his siblings eventually anyway. Parsifal was just spending what would be his a bit sooner, that's all.

But then something happened. And, because it was a dream, a double-dream, what should have taken months happened in milliseconds.

There was something called a Depression, and as Parsifal walked down the main street of the town he saw that all the shops were empty, there were beggars lying in the street begging for money or bread, and huge queues had formed outside the shops—but there was nothing to buy. Parsifal recognized some of his friends in the queues and went over to say hello. But when they found out he had no gold rings left they weren't interested in being his friends anymore. Parsifal stood on the pavement and shook the silk purse inside out. But it was completely empty, apart from a moth. Even the moth flew away in disgust.

Suddenly Parsifal felt frightened. What would he do? One of his now ex-friends told him to try doing some work for a living.

Work? That was the very thing he'd been trying to avoid. If he had wanted to work he might as well have stayed on the farm. But here he was, stuck in this town with no money. So Parsifal started to look for a job. And because this was a dream, a double-dream, he knew immediately that there was only one job left in the whole town. And he was so weary and hungry he would have to do it, even though it was the ultimate humiliation for a pig.

He was going to have to be the servant of a human being.

Parsifal hated human beings. They were horrible creatures who had always been horrible to him. Words could not express the contempt he felt for the hired hands on the farm who were supposed to be looking after all the animals. They had been incompetent and nasty and would probably kill you as soon as look at you.

Parsifal found himself standing outside a dirty old building with a sign that read: 'HELP WANTED: Female Secretary. Must be able to type and write. Will be paid in Real Money. APPLY WITHIN'.

Real money. That was what he needed to survive in this awful town. He could write well enough. But what was typing? And they wanted a female. That was pushing things a bit.

As if to complete his humiliation, Parsifal looked down and discovered that he was wearing a dress, high-heeled shoes and lace gloves. He sighed and rang the doorbell.

'And what type of typist are you?' were the words that greeted Parsifal as he was shown into an office on the ground floor. The speaker must have been Mr Orwell, for that was the name on the door.

'Oh, er, Mr Orwell, sir,' Parsifal stammered in a high-pitched voice, trying to sound like his sister Parsley, 'I'm sure I'm the very sort of typist you're looking for.'

'You're a bit fat, aren't you? How are you going to sit on my knee?' guffawed the man behind the desk. He had large dark eyes, a gaunt white face, and a small toothbrush moustache. 'I need someone to inspire me, you know, to be my muse, for a book I'm trying to write. Can you be my muse?'

What was a muse? Parsifal had never heard of this animal before. It sounded like a combination between a mew and a moo—perhaps it was some strange cross between a cat and a cow?

'Please, sir,' said Parsifal. 'I'm desperate. I'll be anything you want, do anything you want, as long as I can get something to eat!'

At that moment his stomach gave the longest and loudest growl it had ever made. Mr Orwell smiled.

'Can you take dictation?' he asked.

Dictation? What dictation? Parsifal suddenly felt angry and afraid. 'I'm not going to be dictated to by anybody!' he declared stoutly (even though he hadn't eaten for so long that he was a bit thinner by this time).

Mr Orwell began to laugh. He laughed, and laughed, and laughed.

'Oh, ho ho, a revolting pig! Ha, ha, ha! Wonderful! A pig that won't be dictated to by human beings!' He continued to laugh as Parsifal stood there with his trotters on his hips, scowling at his potential employer. Then the man went quiet, as if something had struck him.

'Yee-ees, yee-ees, that should do it,' he murmured. He began to scribble something down on his notepad. 'A revolt of the animals. An animals' revolution. A pig on hind legs. Hmm. Yes, that's it!' Mr Orwell looked up at Parsifal. 'I think you've been my muse after all!'

He stood up and walked Parsifal over to the door.

'I think you should probably go home,' Mr Orwell said. 'This big town is no place for little pigs. It's a cruel place built by human beings for human beings. Believe me, I know. Go back to the Animal Farm where you belong.'

And with that he slipped a silver coin into Parsifal's lace lady's glove—enough to get him back safely to Far Off Farm. At that moment Parsifal suddenly came to his senses. On the farm he had friends, he always had enough to eat, and his family was waiting for him. He snuffled a bit as he remembered how worried his parents would be about his disappearance.

'Thank you very much, Mr Orwell,' Parsifal said as he left the great man's office. 'I'll do as you say.'

'Call me George,' said the man as he waved goodbye.

And because this was a dream, a double-dream, in no time at all Parsifal was back at Far Off Farm, climbing up the path that led to the sty where his parents would be. What would his father do? What would his mother say? Would they be pleased to see him or angry? Would they even speak to him at all? He'd have to offer to do all the chores in the sty for ever more to make up for his bad behaviour. How could he ever make up for stealing his father's gold rings and his mother's silk purse?

As the sty came into sight, Parsifal could see his father leaning over the fence, scanning the horizon. Parsifal gulped.

The boar had stopped turning his head and was now looking in Parsifal's direction. He'd been spotted.

Then the boar started throwing himself at the fence, trying to launch himself over it. Parsifal shuddered. He must be really mad. Next the boar began trying to knock the fence down, battering himself against it over and over again. Should Parsifal just take to his trotters and run in the opposite direction? He was in for it now. He could just imagine how sore his bottom was going to be after the beating he was going to get.

His father finally managed to knock part of the fence down and came hurtling down the path towards Parsifal. It was all the little pig could do to stand still and not faint or flee. He steeled himself for the impact of the first blow.

And he was indeed practically knocked down—by the force of his father's huge embrace. The boar picked Parsifal up and swung him round and covered him in kisses.

'I'm ... I'm so sorry, F...f...father,' gasped the little pig. 'I've been a very bad little pig. Please forgive me.'

'You're forgiven,' the boar murmured into his ear. 'I'm just glad you're alive and well.' He held his son at arm's length for a moment. 'Are those human high heels you're wearing? Never mind, come in and I'll tell your mother and brother and sister you're safe and we'll have a big party!'

The boar carried Parsifal back into the sty on his shoulders in triumph. His mother came out of the shed and threw herself, weeping, against her son's legs.

'Get out the last of the parsnip wine!' cried her husband. 'And heat up the larkspit bark! My son was lost, but now he's found!'

But, on the other side of the sty, Parsnip and Parsley, Parsifal's older brother and sister, were working hard at their chores. They looked up to see what all the noise was about and were amazed to see their lost younger brother, the prodigal pig, on their father's shoulders. As if he'd just won a race or a prize! That was hardly fair now, was it?

They took one look at each other, wiped the sweat off their foreheads, rolled up the fat on their arms, and stormed over to where their mother and father were doing a little dance with Parsifal.

'What's all this?' demanded Parsnip, the oldest little pig.

'And who is this?' cried Parsley, pointing at the exhausted but happy Parsifal.

'Don't be silly,' said their mother. 'It's your little brother. He's come back to us. Isn't it wonderful?'

'We don't have a little brother anymore,' said Parsnip.

'Unless you're referring to the little rat who stole our inheritance and wasted it on loose living in the big town and treated us as if we were of no account,' said Parsley. 'Even if that lowest-of-the-low did come back, I wouldn't speak to him. He's no longer worthy of our love.'

Parsley flounced off, followed by Parsnip. Even their tails curled aggressively as they turned their backs on their brother.

'Dear Parsnip, dear Parsley!' cried their father as he rushed after them. 'Please don't act like this. We all need to forgive him. Can't you see how wonderful it is? Your little brother was lost, and now he's found. We feared he might be dead, but he's alive and kicking. And we're all reunited as a family. That's worth more than any gold ring or silk purse. Isn't having your brother alive worth more than a dead bit of metal or material? I know you'd already seen yourselves wearing those nose and earrings and using that purse when your mother and I are dead and gone but...'

The two little pigs protested, half-heartedly.

'... and perhaps you were even stealing them in your mind's eye,' their father continued, 'and wishing us dead is as bad in the end as what your little brother actually did.'

Parsnip and Parsley hung their heads in shame.

'So let's not worry about tomorrow,' their father urged. 'Let's make the most of today. You two have always been with me and your mother, and we can still enjoy each other's company. Take a day off from your chores—let's have a big party!'

Parsnip and Parsley looked at each other and sighed, then they nodded their heads. They smiled and trotted behind their father to join in the hugs and kisses.

As the five of them danced around that night in the light of the stars, laughing after too much parsnip wine and larkspit bark, Parsifal felt as if they had danced right up out of the sty and into the sky. As he was swung round, his trotters flailing into the air, it was as if the Big Pig himself had joined them and was wheeling them round in an endless celestial reel.

When Parsifal woke up, he found that his trotters had left the pedals of the Dream Cycle. He was waving them around in mid-air with only the handlebars for support in the battle with gravity. Gravity won, and he came to earth with the proverbial bump—fortunately on a part of his rump that was better padded than it was supposed to be. He lay on his back in the health farm gym, grinned, and closed his eyes. If only he could wish himself asleep and be back in that merry dance with his family and the Big Pig again. If only it could come true. Then he would be perfectly happy.

Parsifal tried to get up and stumbled. He looked down. No wonder he had fallen off the Dream Cycle. For on his bottom trotters were human high-heeled shoes.

14

The Street Rat and the Night Shift

Parsifal could hardly wait for the next night to arrive. After another exhausting day working out in the gym, the slightly-more-little pig took up his usual post on the Dream Cycle in order to get himself in the right state of mind to sleep. As the wheels began to hum and whir, Parsifal found himself becoming sleepier and sleepier.

And soon he began to dream.

In his dream, his double-dream, Parsifal was walking down a dark alley in a dark town on a dark night. He had never seen the alley or the town before (since he had always lived on a farm, this is hardly surprising). It was so dark that he couldn't tell what he was walking on or treading in. It was raining and windy, and he was wet, but he was also covered in sweat as if he had just been running or cycling. But where was he running to—or what was he running from?

There was a street light up ahead, shining faintly in the gloom at the end of the narrow alley. Suddenly Parsifal realized that he was not alone. The darkness round him had come to life with long wheezing breaths, vicious whispers with no words.

He started to run. He ran and ran and ran.

But because it was a dream, a double-dream, his trotters made no progress. Rain blew down on him, and then sharp blows rained down on him. The muggers, whoever they were, made off with his full wallet, a smart paisley waistcoat, and a gold watch-and-chain that Parsifal hadn't even known he had—as well as a rather smart porkpie hat that he had apparently been wearing.

Parsifal was left lying in the gutter. He struggled to raise himself up on one trotter. Through swollen eyes, he could see the silhouettes of a gang of hyenas and weasels disappearing round the far corner of the alley, where a dim light glimmered.

Then he fell backwards with a thump, bruising his aching head. What should he do?

The rain came down harder. This was no gentle rain that he could imagine to be tears of sympathy but a contemptuous rain, pelting down on him, hammering on his bruises and mingling with the blood from his wounds. How long this went on, he had no idea.

But then a car turned into the alley and drove to where Parsifal was lying. Through his swollen eyelids, he could see that it was a sleek pink limousine, stretched to the length of several houses. It drove through a puddle as it pulled up next to him, splattering him with mud.

One of the black-tinted windows of the limousine glided down with an electronic sigh. Out of the window peered a haughty white poodle wearing a strapless satin ball gown, a diamond tiara, and a ruby collar. The Rich Bitch gazed at Parsifal in horror, holding her paws up to her face and flapping her false eyelashes.

'Oh, what a revolting pig!' she yapped. 'What a terrible mess he is in! Drive on, Driver, drive on! He might get blood

Drive on, Driver, drive on!

on my new ball gown! He might mug us and I'm wearing my best jewellery! Drive on, Driver, drive on!'

Before Parsifal could even moan, she had whirred up her window again and the limo had screeched off into the night, splattering Parsifal with mud as it left. He sank back into the gutter, feeling every one of his bruises. Was there no one to help him? How long would he have to lie here before someone took pity on him?

Now a roaring sound came down the alley. It grew louder and louder. A huge mass of shining black and silver metal came to a shuddering stop near Parsifal.

'Hey, man, I didn't see you there,' cried the leather-clad biker. 'Are you trying to get yourself killed?'

The rider took off his black-tinted helmet and Parsifal saw that it was a dalmatian in a white dog collar. It was a trendy vicar dog, hurrying on his way to a service.

'I'd offer you a ride, but I'd be late for our alternative service and I'm the key speaker. You should come along sometime. We meet in the old warehouse. We get hundreds of young animals along to worship the Top Dog. They wouldn't go anywhere else! We present the Top Dog as a Dog in our image, one the young pups can really relate to! It's great for them to know that the Big Animal is just the same as them really! We have megawatts of music from the best sound system around! And we preach complete self-acceptance and self-love! Come exactly as you are—we won't try and change you, just give you a great time! You'll love it! Anyhow, I must rush—can't let them start without me! Hope to see you there, brother! Stay cool!'

And the Reverend Dalmatian put on his tinted helmet, revved up his engine, and sped off into the night with a screech of his wheels. Parsifal gazed at the sky and shivered in the cool night air. He had no hope. If even a vicar in a dog collar wouldn't help him, who would? He said he worshipped the Big Animal (or the 'Top Dog' as he called him). What was wrong? Why didn't the Big Animal send someone who could help him?

In his dream, his double-dream, Parsifal faded in and out of consciousness a few times before the next animal came along. This time, the first thing Parsifal became aware of was a high-pitched metallic *'greep-greep-greep-greep'*. It reminded him of the sound of the hired hands on Far Off Farm sharpening their long knives on a stone wheel before killing an animal. The excruciating sound was getting closer and closer and louder and louder. Parsifal wanted to put his trotters in his ears. He couldn't bear it any more. If someone was sharpening a knife and coming to kill him— let them. Better to die quickly than to suffer a lingering death in the gutter.

Just when Parsifal thought he could take no more of the *'greep-greep-greeping'*, it stopped. He forced open one swollen eye and looked up.

What stood in front of him made his blood run cold. The animal he hated most. His worst fear come true.

It was a rat. An enormous rat. An enormous ugly street rat.

There is nothing worse than a rat—except a street rat. They don't even have the decency to live on a farm. They are so lost to civilization that they live in the gutters of the cities and survive on the dirt and filth that others throw away. Street rats slink down into the sewers of the cities and bathe in excrement and urban bile. Street rats have no friends—and they don't want any. A street rat is a byword for the lowest of the low. They survive by violence, theft and stealth.

Parsifal hated rats. Even on Far Off Farm he had hated them. All the animals did, for the rats would sneak up on families at night and make off with their babies in the darkness. The half-eaten bodies of the young would be found the next morning, left as appalling reminders of the murders that had taken place. Parsifal knew that his parents had lost other children from previous litters to these swift and silent killers.

'Oh, please,' gasped Parsifal, closing his eyes again as if in prayer. 'Make it quick! Please just do it quickly! I want it to be over with quickly. Kill me now, don't make me wait!'

There was silence for a while.

Then he heard a loud hiccup.

Parsifal opened one eye suspiciously. Was the street rat drunk?

The street rat tottered forward a few paces and nearly fell on top of Parsifal. He reeked of alcohol. Parsifal could hardly catch his breath for the smell—that and the fact that this very large rat had just trodden on one of his trotters. With a great deal of snuffling and sighing and inarticulate mumbling and grumbling, the street rat walked round behind Parsifal, bent down, put his arms under Parsifal's armpits and, with a great heave, tried to lift him up. Parsifal was choked with fear. Was this the prelude to being garrotted or strangled or suffocated? The stink of the street rat's mangy fur alone could probably kill at twenty paces.

It was then that Parsifal noticed the shopping trolley. It was battered and broken and had a bit of old carpet, a stack of wet newspapers, and a lot of empty bottles in it. He realized that the street rat was trying to put him in the trolley along with the other detritus he had been collecting from the gutter that night. Perhaps the street rat was part of a gang, and Parsifal would be one of the trophies that he would take back to his lair—to share the killing with his comrades. Parsifal's imagination, fuelled by panic, went into overdrive.

But the street rat couldn't lift Parsifal. So he wandered over to the shopping trolley, pushed it over onto its side—scattering bottles and newspapers in the process—and slid it over to where Parsifal was lying. This made a hideous metallic screeching. When the trolley was as close to Parsifal as it would go, the rat got behind the pig again and pushed and pushed as hard as he could. And Parsifal pushed and pushed as hard as he could—in the opposite direction. But Parsifal soon gave up. Why not co-operate and let death come as quickly as possible? He could only hope that the gang of rats wouldn't torture him first.

With an almighty effort the street rat lifted the trolley upright again, this time with the prostrate pig inside. After taking a moment to catch his breath, the rat set off pushing the trolley down the dark alley. To Parsifal's horror, he heard the 'greep-greep-greep' sound again—but then he realized it was only the sound of a broken wheel on the shopping trolley, and not a knife being sharpened.

It took a while for the rat to steer the trolley to the end of the alley. Because of its broken wheel, the trolley kept veering to the left and the rat, muttering, had to keep dragging it back onto the right track again. Where were they going? Parsifal blacked out.

Out of the alley, down another alley, and then left down another, and the rat and his unusual burden arrived at the main street of the town. There, lit up in lurid neon, was a motel with a gaudy sign, 'Rest Your Wheels Here'. It took the street rat a few minutes to push the trolley through the traffic and across the street. Impatient motorists swore at him and cuffed the back of his head as he passed.

Once they were in the grubby lobby of the motel, the rat fumbled around inside a plastic bag in the trolley for some money. At last he found some coins and notes, extracted them from the chewing gum and cold greasy chips that had somehow got wrapped up with them, and handed the money to a weasel who sat smoking behind the counter. The weasel nodded, gave the rat a room key, and waved a paw in the direction of the lift.

'Aaahhh!' Parsifal awoke to shooting pain all through his body. It was his cry of agony and alarm that brought him round. Was this the torture he had feared?

But the street rat was bathing Parsifal's wounds. He had taken the (rather grubby) flannel from the motel sink, soaked it in some sort of raw alcohol as an antiseptic, and was dabbing the flannel on some of Parsifal's worst wounds. Parsifal had to grit his teeth to stop from crying out again. But each time the rat lifted the flannel off, Parsifal felt as if his skin could breathe again. Although the wounds were still sore, the worst was over. When the rat was finished Parsifal wanted to croak out a 'thank you', but he was too choked up to speak.

Then the rat ripped up one of the sheets from the bed to use as bandages. He folded the strips into pads, put some ointment on them, and placed them on Parsifal's worst wounds. This stung terribly too, but the pain wasn't quite as bad as before. Now that Parsifal understood that the rat was trying to help him, he was determined to be brave and not make a fuss. Next the rat took a tin of sticking plaster out of his trolley and opened it with difficulty. Balancing the tin on his left foot, he pulled up a long length of sticking plaster, most of which stuck to his fur. Parsifal cringed as he watched the rat pull the plaster off his mangy fur, taking quite a few chunks of the fur with it. Eventually the rat mastered the correct technique with the plaster and secured the pig's pads and bandages. Then Parsifal panicked as he realized that the rat was about to leave. Tears sprang to his eyes.

'Oh, don't go!' he cried in a hoarse voice. 'I haven't thanked you! How can I thank you enough?'

The rat dismissed this with a wave of his paw and began to leave the room—but not without knocking over a chamber pot and a row of bottles that had been left in the way.

It was only then that Parsifal realized that the rat had been injured too. There was blood on the rat's four paws and a deep wound in his side. The rat had also been attacked and injured, but he had taken all this time and effort to look after Parsifal first. Parsifal felt more tears springing to his eyes—this time not from his own pain. Now he understood that the rat hadn't been drunk. It had been so knocked about that it could hardly walk straight. It had smelled of alcohol because the gang had doused it in alcohol as a prelude to setting it alight. Parsifal could see all this clearly in his mind's eye as he lifted a trotter in silent thanks. As the door closed on the scuzzy back of the street rat, a breeze blew through the room and flapped the curtain. In place of the smell of alcohol and worse, there came to Parsifal's nostrils the irresistible smell of summer roses.

As Parsifal fell asleep in the motel, he awoke in the gym. He was still at the health farm. He had fallen off the

Dream Cycle and had several throbbing bruises and a cut on one leg. But instead of panicking, he lay on his back and thought for a bit. He thought of the street rat—someone he had thought of as an enemy who had turned out to be his greatest friend and saviour.

Then Parsifal thought of the Big Animal.

And instead of the odour of sweat and strong cologne that usually hung in the air in the gym, it seemed to Parsifal that the air was full of the sweet smell of summer roses.

15

The Big Party

This became Parsifal's daily routine at the health farm. He would wake up at some unearthly hour of the morning after a strange double-dream and then not be able to go back to sleep again. He would lie there for a couple of hours, thinking about the Big Animal, his own failure, and his need for forgiveness. And he would relish the sense of the Big Animal's presence with which each of the double-dreams left him. It gave him the strength to go through the exhausting daily routine of exercise and strict diet. Every week the Catechism Cat would take his measurements, usually with her lips curled in disdain. Then one week she actually began to smile as she wrote his measurements down on a chart.

There were a few weeks when Parsifal had no significant dreams at all. He had been so tired each night that he had just fallen into bed without his usual stint on the Dream Cycle and had slept in sweet oblivion until dawn.

But then one night he decided to give it another go. He sneaked into the gym when all the other animals were asleep and sat on the Dream Cycle again. As he began to pedal, he was amazed at how much easier it was now that he was so much fitter. He could get up to speed very quickly. And soon he was snoring rhythmically in time with the whir of the wheels and was sinking into the domain of the double-dream.

In his dream, his double-dream, Parsifal was lying on his back in front of his fireplace at home. His back legs were cycling in the air as he read an invitation he was holding in his front trotters.

The invitation was printed on an expensive white card with gold-edging and read

His Supreme and Almighty Majesty
THE BIG ANIMAL
requests the pleasure of the company of
Parsifal the Pilgrim Pig
at
THE PARTY TO END ALL PARTIES
at the Big Posh Banqueting Hall.
Black Tie (Be there—or else!)

The invitation also gave the date and the time of the Party to End All Parties. Parsifal glanced over at the calendar that hung on the wall. The date was today! He looked at this watch. The time was now! The party was on right now. And he wasn't ready. If he didn't leave this very second he was going to be late.

Parsifal ran upstairs, jumped in and out of the shower (without turning it on), wrapped a black cloth around his neck (it used to be white, but now it was black and would have to do for a tie) and ran back down the stairs. As he did so, he tripped over several tin plates of leftover food which clattered like the percussion section of an orchestra gone mad. He flung open the front door, slammed the front door, and leapt on a bicycle that he didn't know he possessed that happened to be standing on the porch. He pedalled and pushed and sweated and pedalled. But he wasn't getting anywhere. The cycle seemed to be attached to the porch. This was a good thing, as Parsifal had forgotten his invitation. He flung open the door again, grabbed the gold-edged invitation, and this time when he began to pedal wildly the cycle began to move. It didn't stop until he was at the entrance to the Big Posh Banqueting Hall.

Parsifal tottered up to the massive doorway, weak at the knees and faint in the head. Gasping and panting, he handed his invitation to the very posh penguin who was standing guard at the door. The penguin looked him up and down with raised eyebrows. He sniffed loudly, put on a pair of half-moon glasses that were hanging round his neck on a chain, and examined the invitation minutely. With a sharp intake of breath, he smoothed back his oiled fringe with one wing and said, 'It appears to be genuine enough. I suppose I will have to let you in, though you are a revolting pig!'

The penguin sniffed again and looked down his beak as Parsifal gabbled his thanks and launched himself at the door of the Big Posh Banqueting Hall.

This was the wrong thing to do. Parsifal had not noticed that the large gold and glass door was a revolving door. Instead of making his grand entrance into the hall, Parsifal found himself in an enclosed glass cabinet that spun him round and round and then flung him out onto the steps again, where he fell at the feet of the posh penguin and the guests who were waiting to enter. This happened several times. Each time the penguin pushed Parsifal in, out he would fly—knocking down the other guests like skittles in a bowling alley. As they struggled to their feet and rubbed their bruises, some of them began to call Parsifal names— not only was he a *revolting* pig, but also a *revolving* pig.

Finally, with the help of a whole row of whelks who joined him inside the revolving door and pushed him out at the right moment, Parsifal was at last inside. But then his real problems began.

He was awestruck by the beautiful entrance of the Big Posh Banqueting Hall. He looked up at the gold-leaf ceiling made with real golden leaves, at the crystal chandeliers hung with real crystal tinkling tears. He looked down at the red carpet with a pile so thick it almost covered his trotters. Another penguin ushered him through another doorway (fortunately there was no door this time) into the main ballroom where the party was to take place. Here there were marble columns, marble fountains and marble statues. As Parsifal walked through the doorway, two liveried armadillos stood to attention and loudly announced, 'PARSIFAL THE PILGRIM PIG!'

Parsifal took a few tentative steps down a grand golden staircase into the ballroom itself. His eyes were caught by the starry sapphire and diamond ceiling. He gazed up in amazement—and missed his step. Next moment, he was rolling rump over trotter down twenty more. But the stars in his eyes only made the scene more beautiful. He got up, brushed himself off, and looked with a dopey gaze at all the other animals, who were all looking at him. They were all wearing beautiful outfits—glittering ball gowns or black suits with stiff white shirts and black ties.

It was only then in his dream, his double-dream, that Parsifal realized he was supposed to be wearing clothes. He had assumed that the words 'Black Tie' on the invitation meant just that—he was supposed to wear a black tie ... and nothing else.

Parsifal fervently hoped that the other guests hadn't noticed. He sidled off to a table loaded with food and tried to hide his embarrassment behind two carefully placed mushroom vol-au-vents and a truffle surprise. But it was no use.

A giraffe (who had been straining her neck and using opera glasses to get a better look) was the first to voice her concern over his condition. Her cry was as long as it was loud. 'Aaahhh!' (Giraffes have very large lungs.) 'It's disgusting! He's *completely* naked—apart from that *filthy* black rag round his neck. Get him *out* of here—he's not fit to be seen by *respectable* animals!' She then proceeded to lean to one side in slow motion, as if fainting from shock.

Then everyone else joined in.

'It's disgusting!'

'How dare he?'

'What an outrage!'

'He's not wearing the right clothes!'

And then, in unison, they all cried out, 'What a revolting pig!'

Before he knew what was happening in his dream, his double-dream, the poor pig had an armed armadillo on each arm hustling him out of the room and a posh penguin panting after him. 'We really must ask you to leave!'

'B...b...but the B...B...Big Animal invited me!' Parsifal stammered as the armadillos carried him back up the golden stairs. He could have wept. They were right. He didn't belong here. The hall was buzzing with the murmuring and whispering of all the other animals and he knew that what they were saying was true. He wasn't properly dressed— there was no denying it.

But, just as the armadillos were about to fling him out of the ballroom, all the murmuring stopped as if it had been switched off. There was a clap of thunder and flash of lightning. The armadillos and the penguin turned round, their faces pale, and flung themselves down on the floor. All the other animals did the same.

For there, in a blinding shaft of light, stood the Big Animal himself.

Parsifal felt the floor quaking beneath his trotters. He wasn't sure whether that was because of the presence of the Big Animal or whether it was the trembling of all the other animals now prostrate before him.

To Parsifal's horror, the Big Animal spoke in a thunderous voice, 'BRING THE PIG TO ME!'

Why, oh why, had he dared to come to the Big Animal's Party to End All Parties dressed only in a filthy rag? What was the Big Animal going to do to him?

As the armadillos dragged Parsifal into the great shining light of the Big Animal's presence, he closed his eyes and hoped for the best. It was all he could do.

The armadillos flung the pig down before the Big Animal and withdrew. Parsifal was blinded by the light that seemed to be surrounding or coming from the Big Animal. It was just as the Big Animal had told him all that time ago on their first evening in the new house. It was impossible for animals to see what the Big Animal was like in himself. They could only see him when he took a form like theirs. But for some reason, at the Party to End All Parties, the Big Animal had chosen to appear in all his glory. Perhaps, Parsifal thought, it was because this Party really was going to be the Last—the Last Party ever held on earth. Parsifal gulped.

Though the heat and light were almost unbearable, what was more unbearable still was the sheer power of the love that the Big Animal was pouring over Parsifal's mind and body. Parsifal wanted to cry and cry and cry. Somehow he knew that the Big Animal could see all the things he had ever done wrong—and still loved him anyway. And wasn't that the message that the Big Pig had left for Parsifal? 'REMEMBER YOU ARE LOVED. THAT'S ALL YOU NEED TO KNOW (FOR NOW)'.

'I'm s...s...sorry,' sobbed the little pig. 'I'm sorry I've come to your party in the wrong clothes. All I have is this filthy rag and I can't even cover myself with that. I have nothing to offer you. I'm not worthy to be at your party. I deserve to be thrown out.'

And Parsifal began to weep in overwhelming despair. Now that he could feel the Big Animal's love for him again, the last thing he wanted was to be thrown out of his presence.

But something very strange happened. Instead of throwing him out of the Big Banqueting Hall and into the dark, to weep and gnash his teeth for evermore, the Big Animal encircled Parsifal with his cloak. And immediately Parsifal was wearing a tuxedo—a jet-black suit, a snow-white shirt (Snow White had washed and ironed it herself), and a very smart black tie! The black evening coat even had penguin tails at the back, just as smart as those worn by the penguin at the door.

This was no ordinary suit. It was a suit that belonged to the Big Pig himself. The Big Animal was lending Parsifal his own beautiful and perfectly cut clothes so that Parsifal could stay at his party and be in his presence. Parsifal would have hugged the Big Animal if he had known how to hug this enormous Being of Light. Instead, as if the Big Animal could read Parsifal's thoughts, a very large and perfectly manicured trotter appeared out of the light. It was the Big Pig's trotter! At last Parsifal could touch the Big Animal again. Parsifal knelt down and kissed and snuffled against the immaculate trotter held out to him in welcome.

At this sign of the Big Animal's grace, all the other animals at the party cheered and applauded, whistled and hooted, whinnied and roared. Even the cats called out their approval.

'ALRIGHT EVERYONE,' the Big Animal declared, 'LET'S PARTY!'

Parsifal found himself being spun round by a lady pig in a sequined dress, and soon, instead of tripping up, he was stepping out in a strictly ballroom style of dancing. All the other animals were whirling around in perfect unity. The great light of the Big Animal's presence ricocheted off the crystal chandeliers, sprinkling the dance floor with shades of red, orange, yellow, green, blue and violet. Beautiful music kept them all dancing in time. And Parsifal forgot all about food.

In his dream, his double-dream, Parsifal threw back his head and laughed, and as he did so he fell off the Dream Cycle in the gym at the health farm. The whirling went on, but now it was inside his poor head as he came to with a bump on the floor. All that remained was a huge and hungry longing—not for mushroom vol-au-vents or truffle surprises, but for the Big Animal, and for all the other animals who had been with him at the Last Dance.

As he remembered that wonderful night, Parsifal knew, in a strange, slow intuition, that the Party to End All Parties was yet to come. He had yet to take his partner in the Last Dance.

It was morning. It must have rained during the night, for as Parsifal looked up and out of the windows of the gym, he saw that a rainbow graced the grey sky.

16

Pig Sick

I n all these weeks, Parsifal Pig had never left the health farm. So he could hardly believe his ears when the Catechism Cat announced that tomorrow Parsifal and a few of his friends were to go on something called a 'mission' to another farm. It took a while to work this out because the Catechism Cat wasn't good at pronouncing any word beginning with the letter 'M'. The animals knew that they just had to be patient until she managed to spit it out. The best they could hope for was that, in her frustration, she wouldn't spit at them! It usually came out something like *'M...m...mi...mi...miiiiiiAAOOOWW—oh drat!'* At first Parsifal and his friends had wondered what a 'Miaow-o-drat' was and whether it would hurt much (most things that the Catechism Cat told them to do hurt quite a bit).

Finally the cat could stand their stupidity no longer. She wrote the word in the sand in her tray so they could all read it. But even then they were none the wiser. What on earth was a 'mission'?

The cat shook her head. 'Didn't they teach you *anything* at your farms? A m...m...m—you know, is when you go to another farm, like the Far Off Farms you've come from, and tell them all about the health farm and getting fit for the Purrrfect Farm,' the cat explained. 'You take your before-and-after photos and illustrate how you became fit on some portable keep-fit equipment. Then you let the animals you meet on the farms have a go. It's simple. Aaall you have to do is tell them the good news about the health farm and what you now know about the Big Animal. It's your experience of him that's the important bit and you sort of give a testimony about it. It's easy. A slug could do it. Slugs have done it. Even a pig can do it.' As she said this, she cast a mean look at a Parsifal, who was looking a bit shaky.

Go to other farms? Show them his before-and-after photos? Give a testimony? Talk about his experiences of the Big Animal in public? Tomorrow?

Parsifal didn't sleep much that night. He didn't dare use the Dream Cycle, so he spent the night in a cramped cubicle in the changing room. He hoped he would oversleep and be overlooked when the time came to leave the next morning.

At three o'clock in the morning, however, he was still wide awake with a stomach ache. It couldn't be anything he'd eaten because he hadn't eaten anything. He hadn't been able to eat with this mission-thing hanging over him. He felt his forehead with one trotter. Was that sweat? Was he feverish? Perhaps if he was ill he wouldn't have to go on this mission-thing and bare his soul (and body) to lots of strange animals who probably didn't want to listen to him anyway.

Parsifal was particularly embarrassed at the thought of other animals seeing his before-and-after photos. In the 'after' one he looked pretty good now, with his muscles primed and pumped up, but he was only wearing a small flannel strategically held in place by the Catechism Cat (you could see her paw extending across from the left-hand side of the frame). And as for the 'before' photo—well, Parsifal didn't even want to think about it. It was awful to be reminded of how he'd let himself go to pot (especially his belly) when he had started to be self-indulgent and had taken the Big Pig's friendship for granted.

And what was this testimony thing anyway? Anything with the word 'test' in it sounded worrying. Was he going to have to go into embarrassing detail about how he had left his house and made a complete fool of himself on the way to the health farm?

He told himself to stop thinking about these things. If he didn't get some sleep, he wouldn't be fit for anything in the morning—not even putting on a convincing show of being too ill to go on this mission-thing.

Parsifal closed his eyes tight. He frowned. Something was tickling his arm. It was his other arm. He coughed. Something was tickling his ear. It was his arm again. Why couldn't his body just settle down and relax? It was as if his flesh had a mind of its own. He felt strange itching sensations all over. He twitched his snout and told his flesh to calm down. He was going to get to sleep if it killed him.

But then, out of nowhere (and no, this wasn't a double-dream), a cold breeze began to blow. At first it was faint, but then it grew stronger and stronger. Soon the wooden door of the cubicle began swinging open and closed in an uneven rhythm. Had someone left a window open?

Parsifal sighed and prised his eyelids open. He could just make out a small patch of slightly lighter darkness each time the door flapped open. It was still early morning. Everything else was black. The tiny bit of light was coming from the windows high up near the ceiling in the changing room.

Parsifal wondered what time it was. He held up one trotter and squinted. Could he see it yet? Yes, he could just about make out its shape when it was a foot or so from his face. He decided it must be nearly four o'clock. Parsifal was just about to force his eyelids shut again when something very mysterious began to happen.

A strong gust of cold wind came from nowhere and blew the door off the cubicle. It flew off its hinges and clattered to the floor. Parsifal sat bolt upright, his eyes as round as wagon wheels. Was he in a double-dream ... or was this *really* happening? He gulped.

Before Parsifal's startled eyes, all the darkest bits of darkness in the room, all the blackest bits of black, all the shadiest bits of shade, rushed together from every corner. With a sickening whoosh they massed together into one huge and terrifying shape. The Night Mare!

She seemed to fill the changing room. Her black mane and tail whipped around, as if she was standing in a high wind (which she was). She pawed the ground, snorting and shaking her head, as if Parsifal had just opened his mouth and said entirely the wrong thing.

Parsifal opened his mouth. The Night Mare glared at him. Parsifal shut his mouth. The Night Mare's green eyes flared as if lit by an evil flame. Try as he might, Parsifal could not take his eyes off her. Was this what it felt like to be hypnotized?

'You will come with me,' said the Night Mare without moving her lips. The sound of her eerie voice turned his trotters to water.

Even though Parsifal felt that he couldn't move if he tried, he found himself floating upwards. His blanket fell away. He was being inexorably drawn towards the Night Mare. Now the strong cold wind forced open the windows of the changing room, and the Night Mare flew upwards and out through the window, sucking Parsifal out behind her. He found himself flying through the night air at tremendous speed in her smoking, choking black wake.

The Night Mare looked back at him and Parsifal could feel her breath flecked with flame, as she said, 'Now I am going to see what you are made of!'

Parsifal could have told her. He was made of jelly! Then he made a mistake. He looked down. And suddenly he saw all the suffering in the world. There beneath him in the darkness lay farm after farm after farm on which all the animals were howling in pain, calling out for help that would never come. Animals were ill and dying as far as his eye could see. Poverty and suffering reigned supreme. Every single animal was born in pain, scrabbled around in the dirt for a few meaningless years, and was then mercilessly butchered. The horror of this vision gripped Parsifal like a cold hand on his heart.

There was a terrifying lurch and Parsifal realized that they were careering downwards, dropping to the earth like stones. He let out a long, silent shriek, and suddenly they landed. Parsifal was gasping for breath, and his heart was thumping ten times faster than usual.

'Cosmic!' said the Night Mare. 'Wasn't that enjoyable?'

Was the Night Mare on drugs? wondered Parsifal. How could anyone *enjoy* the scenes of suffering they had just flown over? And where were they now? He tried to look around him, but was overcome by coughing as he inhaled the stench that came from the Night Mare. Smoke rolled by like palpable darkness.

As the smoke began to clear, Parsifal looked up. He was amazed to see a beautiful white building before him, with ornate carving and astonishing statues. A golden

The horror...

sign above the enormous doorway read 'THE PALACE OF DELIGHTS'. Underneath, a smaller sign read, 'Come in and have your dreams fulfilled!'

His dreams fulfilled? Parsifal felt a flicker of interest. He wouldn't mind having a look inside to see what was on offer. He had been so good at the health farm. He deserved a bit of a break. All sorts of things he couldn't get at the health farm might be available here. Surely a little self-indulgence couldn't be too awful at this stage? He'd made so much progress that he wouldn't over-indulge again.

And so Parsifal moved, as if hypnotized, towards the Palace of Delights. He became aware that his right ear was itching again, and scratched it with a trotter. What he didn't notice was the Night Mare quickly pulling back her head from close to his side, where she had been whispering thoughts into his mind.

A red carpet had been laid out (especially for him!). Parsifal advanced up the white marble staircase of the Palace of Delights, delighted to see that the guards bowed as if he were royalty as he passed through the great doors. What he didn't see was the wink the Night Mare gave to the guards as she followed him in.

What an amazing place! There was gold and white marble everywhere, and portraits of lordly animals wearing richly decorated clothes. Parsifal couldn't believe his eyes. Even better, he was greeted by a group of beautiful sows wearing diaphanous veils and jewels in their snouts and ears and belly buttons. The most beautiful of them all, with the longest eyelashes, took him by the trotter and led him to a soft satin couch where she offered him a satin-covered box tied with a red ribbon. Undoing the ribbon and opening the box, Parsifal was amazed to see his favourite chocolates. How had this sow known that he liked Peanutbuttermarshmallowfluffcreampuffchocolatetruffle Surprises! He gazed up at her in thanks. She fluttered her eyelashes and began to sway to some music that began very quietly but grew louder as he listened to it, until he too was swaying in time with it as he stuffed his face with chocolates and lay back on the satin couch to watch what would happen next.

The beautiful sow started to dance and to slowly remove one of her seven veils. It fluttered to the ground with a silvery sigh. Parsifal felt the sweat forming on his forehead. Her bangles tinkled as she teasingly fluttered her eyelashes and swayed her hips. She danced close to him, then further away, then close to him again. She seemed to be wearing some sort of crown or tiara. Was she a princess?

Three of the veils were gone now, and as each one fell more and more of the sow's beautiful body was revealed. Parsifal had never seen such a sow before! His mother had never looked like this. His sister had never looked like this. And when they had all danced back on Far Off Farm, it had never been like this!

Parsifal threw his chocolates aside and joined in the dance. He'd be able to help her take off the rest of the veils, if she was having any trouble with them. There were only two left. Parsifal felt his heart was about to explode with excitement. Now the sow was touching him, and leading him towards a tall doorway at one end of the room. She was down to one veil, but she had thrown the last veil over his head so he couldn't see very well. But what he could see through the tall doorway really caught his attention!

There stood twenty golden troughs, filled to overflowing with all of his favourite food. All the wonderful things he hadn't been allowed to eat during his months of deprivation on the health farm. He tore the veil off his head, pushed past the sow (who was about to remove her final veil) and raced for the troughs. He dived head first into the nearest oozing-schmoozing, luscious, delicious load of fodder and proceeded to gulp and snuffle and gulp and snuffle and gulp until he had eaten his way through all twenty troughs. As he lay in the final trough, right next to the tall doorway, he let out an enormous belch of satisfaction. Oh, it was just like old times, feeling his stomach so taut and full—as if he was about to burst.

But what was that noise? It wasn't his stomach rumbling and growling. It wasn't his lungs wheezing with the effort of all that eating. It was something far more sinister. It was the Night Mare laughing.

She had begun by sniggering quietly, but was now in full flow. Her mane tossed and her green eyes blazed and she laughed as if Parsifal had just told the funniest joke in the history of the world.

'I *knew* I could break you!' she whinnied. 'I knew I could get you back! You thought you were so strong after just a few weeks at that health farm. But you were wrong. Just a tiny temptation and you're back to your old self again, troughing away as if there's no tomorrow. And, by the way,' she added with a glint in her eyes, 'there isn't any tomorrow.'

And with that the strong cold wind suddenly began to blow again and the tall doors behind Parsifal blew open with a terrifying BANG!

Parsifal scrabbled round in the golden trough to see what was happening. But then he wished he hadn't.

Yet even if he hadn't looked, he would still have known what he would see, for the room was flooded with the smell that came through the doorway. It was the smell of cooked bacon. Not only cooked bacon, but smoked bacon. Not only cooked bacon, but cooking bacon. And not only bacon, but ham—cooked, smoked and roasted.

The doorway was actually the door of a vast oven, with heaps of glowing coals over which flames played. Hanging above the fire, were the carcasses of many pigs (just like him) who had been butchered. Parsifal vomited up all the food he had just eaten.

'Some people can't resist returning to their old ways,' said the Night Mare with a malicious grin, 'just like a pig returning to its vomit!'

Parsifal looked up at the terrifying black horse. 'Please, please...' he groaned, 'I didn't know—'

'Oh, I think you did,' interrupted the Night Mare. 'And now you belong to me. I can do anything I want with you now—didn't you know that? Wheee, heee, heee, heee! I think you know now! Or did you think that this beautiful sow was going to help you?'

The Night Mare beckoned for the sow to come over to them.

But instead of the beautiful curvaceous sow that had so entranced Parsifal a few moments ago, what he now saw was a hideous warthog, still dressed in one diaphanous veil. Her skin was wrinkled and covered in warts with bristles growing out of them and two vicious tusks sprouted on either side of her snout. If Parsifal had tried to kiss her, he would have had his eyes gouged out! And what had happened to all her beautiful jewellery? All she was wearing now was an iron ankle bracelet attached to a chain pulled by the Night Mare. She was a slave.

As the black horse snorted with glee, Parsifal stared at the warthog with pity and horror.

'What do you think of her now, eh?' cackled the Night Mare. 'Not so pretty in this light, is she? Why don't you two lovebirds—or should I say lovepigs—make a pact to seal your love for ever by jumping into the flames? Go on, I'll even give you a little push, if you like. You could be together for ever, never to be parted—oh, until I hang you up on separate hooks, of course. Oh, wheee, heee, heee, what lovely flitches of bacon you will be!'

And the Night Mare began to push Parsifal towards the terrible doorway, pulling the warthog along by her iron chain. The heat and sulphurous smoke from the furnace were choking and suffocating. A flame licked out and almost singed Parsifal's ear as he tried to get a trotterhold on the smooth marble floor.

'Help! Help!' Parsifal screamed.

The warthog just screamed.

They were both only inches from the doorway of terror and the Oven that Burns Forever.

'Not so fast, Night Mare.'

Who was that?

A quiet, authoritative voice broke through the chaos of noise, smoke, screams and smell. Parsifal realized he was no longer being pushed towards the oven. The Night Mare whinnied hysterically and swung round, lashing Parsifal and the warthog with her tail as she did so. She recognized that voice. It was one she hated and feared.

'Those are my creatures,' said the strong, calm voice, *'not yours.'*

Parsifal slipped and slid in his vomited food as he struggled to turn around and discover who this strange being was who had stopped everything.

It was the Big Pig himself! Parsifal could hardly believe it. Just when he needed him most, the Big Pig, his great friend, had come!

But the Big Pig looked smaller than usual. He didn't look half as impressive as the last time Parsifal had seen him. He was only about Parsifal's size. And he looked rather sad. Parsifal hoped it wasn't because of him.

As the Night Mare whinnied again, Parsifal wondered how the smaller Big Pig was going to stand up to her.

Parsifal tried to run to the Big Pig, but to his horror he found that the Night Mare had slipped an iron slave bracelet onto his ankle too. He was now on the end of a chain controlled by the big black horse.

'They both belong to me!' cried the Night Mare. 'You know the rules. Their souls and bodies are mine and I have the right to cast them into the eternal flames. There's nothing you can do about it—you so-called Almighty Big Animal.' The Night Mare paused to sneer. 'If your creatures choose to disobey you and go their own way, which happens to be my way too, then you have to surrender them to my control.' She jerked the chains, and Parsifal and the warthog fell. They landed still closer to the flaming oven.

'There is still something I can do,' said the Big Pig, more loudly this time.

There was a terrifying pause.

'Oh yeah?' said the Night Mare.

'Take me instead,' said the Big Pig.

Parsifal, the warthog, and the Night Mare all gasped. What was the Big Pig saying? Surely he couldn't mean...

'You ... you ... you...' gibbered the Night Mare, 'you will give your life in exchange for theirs? You must be mad! Wheee, heee, heee, heee!' Her laughter echoed through the chamber.

But suddenly she stopped, and looked panicky—as if she was worried the Big Pig might change his mind. 'Just in case,' she said, and issued a piercing whistle. Immediately another door opened, and in rushed a small army of revolting creatures who had once been weasels, stoats and rats, but who were now so degraded and worn down by evil that they were hardly recognizable. They stood before the Night Mare and waited for her orders. They, too, had slave bracelets on their ankles.

'I have a job for you, my children,' said the Night Mare. She was hardly able to conceal a grin. 'Take this pig here, the so-called Big Pig. Bind him and put him on a spit!'

The weasels, stoats, and rats looked at each other, cowering a little. Who were they more afraid of—the Night Mare or the Big Pig? Things could get nasty for them whichever one they disobeyed.

'Come on, you varlets, you wastrels, you knaves!' cried the Night Mare. 'If you don't, it'll be you in the oven next. I quite fancy fried rat, grilled weasel, or roasted stoat. Don't try my patience, because I don't have any! You must obey me! *Bind the Big Pig and stick him on a spit! We're going to have ourselves a hog roast!*'

With much gibbering and whimpering, the nasty creatures surrounded the Big Pig and began to jab, poke, punch and kick him. He offered no resistance.

'Stop it, stop it!' shouted Parsifal. It was so unfair he wanted to cry.

'And bind those two while you're at it,' ordered the Night Mare. 'I want them to watch their great friend die.

Of course, they'll be next. Once the Big Pig is dead, what's to stop me killing them as well? Wheee, heee, heee, heee!' she laughed as if the idea had only just occurred to her.

The army of rats had completely surrounded the Big Pig, but now they stepped back, giving Parsifal and the warthog a clear view of what had been done to their friend. He was hardly recognizable. He was bruised and bleeding. His eyes were almost swollen shut. And he was roughly bound at all four trotters, trussed up like a slab of meat.

'No!' cried Parsifal. But the weasels and rats grabbed him and the warthog and dragged them back from the flaming doorway to make way for the greater prize.

Parsifal struggled, but there were too many of them, and he was held fast by the chain.

The army of rodents were now busy constructing something. When they had finished, they stepped back and Parsifal could see what it was.

It was a spit. A gigantic roasting spit. A long ugly metal skewer with a handle at one end for turning it on the metal supports. The Night Mare's soldiers lifted the skewer, the shaft of metal glinting in the glow of the fire. Then they advanced on the Big Pig.

Parsifal could not believe what he was seeing. Surely the Big Pig would not allow this? Surely he was too big to lift? But as he watched in horror, four of them forced the skewer through the Big Pig's ankles. The Big Pig cried out twice in pain as he was hoisted onto the metal supports in front of the fire. The slaves uttered cries of delight that they had dared to touch him.

The Big Pig was to have a lingering death, roasting slowly on a spit before the hideous fire.

Parsifal could see no more for his tears. He hid his face in shame and despair. This was his fault. If it hadn't been for his wrongdoing, the Big Pig would not be dying now. The warthog next to him was snuffling too, overcome with grief and pity. Time seemed to stand still. The horrible moment went on and on and on.

Then, suddenly, the Big Pig gave a great cry and, somehow, Parsifal knew that he was gone, killed by the heat and the flames.

The Night Mare gave another maniacal laugh.

'Look and learn, pig,' she said. 'This is what happens to my enemies. Look what I did to your friend. Do you think I won't do the same thing to you? If he could not save himself, how on earth can he save you?'

Then she paused, as if she had second thoughts. 'Just to make sure,' she muttered, and she took up a long fork and thrust it into the side of the Big Pig. She took it out again and inspected it with satisfaction. 'Just wanted to make sure he was done,' she smiled.

Then she yelled to her slaves, 'Take these prisoners to the dungeons!'

Parsifal and his companion were dragged out of the room. He hated to leave the Big Pig, but at least he wouldn't have to see him hung up on a hook or smell his cooking flesh.

Parsifal and the warthog were shoved through the marble hallway, through a dark wooden door, down filthy stone steps, and into a dark underground jail. Hidden under the fancy exterior of the Palace of Delights were row upon row, rank upon rank, of cells. Imprisoned animals peered through the tiny iron grilles in thick wooden doors. All were waiting to die.

Parsifal and the warthog were thrown into a cell and the door was slammed shut.

'We'll deal with you in the morning,' sneered one of the stoats.

Parsifal and the warthog were left all alone. In the darkness they held each other's trotters for comfort and cried. But as he wiped his tears away, Parsifal could see that the warthog's appearance was changing. Her blotchy bristly skin was becoming softer and pinker, like the skin of a newborn piglet, particularly where her tears had run. Many of her warts had been completely washed away, and her tusks were all but gone.

17

Jail Break

When Parsifal opened his eyes the next morning, he desperately hoped that he was going to wake up on the health farm and find that last night had all been a hideous dream. But no. He woke up in the same dark cell where he had been thrown the night before, and the warthog was next to him—although it hardly seemed fair to call her a warthog now. Her warts had completely disappeared and her skin was almost completely new and pink. She was asleep on the cell floor under an old grey blanket.

Parsifal kept quiet so as not to wake her. He thought he had never seen anyone so beautiful. She was snoring lightly and sounding like a real pig. She no longer looked like the enticing sow from yesterday, but in some ways she looked even more beautiful. She had been deeply affected by the Big Pig's death for her, and despite their surroundings she seemed peaceful.

Parsifal's reflections on her transformation were suddenly interrupted by the sound of steps and a jangle of keys. The sow woke up with a cry of fear and sat bolt upright. Parsifal put his arm round her.

But, to Parsifal's surprise, their jailors did not open the door. All they did was light a match outside the grill and let the flame burn briefly while they giggled stupidly. Parsifal and his friend were left wondering what was going on. Why were they just being teased like this? Why hadn't the Night Mare given the order for them to be killed?

On the third day, something very mysterious indeed happened.

Parsifal and the sow woke up as usual. But when their eyes had adjusted to the gloom, they saw that the thick wooden door of their cell was wide open. They looked at each other and then at the door again. What was going on?

'Is it a trap?' whispered the sow. 'Are the soldiers on the other side waiting for us?'

Parsifal gestured for her to be very quiet. He stole over to the door. The lock had been broken—as if someone had blasted it away. Why hadn't the noise woken them up? Parsifal peered round the edge of the doorway into the corridor, looking left and right.

'Nobody there,' he said in surprise.

He beckoned for her to follow, and they crept into the corridor. They kept close to the wall and stopped as they came to the next cell. Its door was also open, and so was the door of the next one, and the next one. In fact, all the cell doors were open, and all the locks were smashed. The animals inside the cell were either still asleep, as Parsifal and the sow had been, or were cowering against the wall inside, too afraid to come out. Parsifal beckoned to them and soon a long file of mice and ducks and squirrels and other pigs had begun to form behind him.

With a gulp he realized that he was at the head of a small army and, if they were to meet the Night Mare's army, there would be a fight.

But as they marched fearfully down the corridor, the Night Mare's hench-animals were nowhere to be found. All that could be seen were a few of their weapons, scattered on the floor as if the soldiers had left in a hurry.

'Let's hope,' whispered Parsifal to the sow, 'that they were fleeing for their lives.'

She nodded, wide eyed.

'What's to stop us going back up to the big hall,' she whispered, 'and seeing what's happened?'

Parsifal gulped again, but he didn't want her to see that he was afraid. So he didn't voice his fear that the whole thing could be a trap, a particularly nasty way for the Night Mare to get all of them as close to the big oven as possible without the effort of doing it herself. He led his small army up the dank stairs and into the main hallway of the Palace of Delights.

Everything was quiet. Parsifal stood on tip-trotter to peer round the door. There was no one in the white marble hallway. The weapons of the Night Mare's army lay scattered around, some of them broken in two. Parsifal wondered whether they should pick them up so that they would be armed if any enemies were still around. But it didn't seem right to use the Night Mare's weapons. They seemed tainted—especially the nasty fork-thing that she had used to pierce the side of the Big Pig. Parsifal thought of it with a shudder and beckoned his troops to gather round him. He addressed them in a hoarse whisper.

'It's possible the Mare is still in there, and her army—we don't know. But it's also possible that they have all fled and we are now in possession of this palace. Whatever the case, I think we should storm the main hall and find out what has happened to ... to ... her latest victim, and make sure that the Big Oven is sealed up so no one can fall in there by mistake. Are you with me?'

The mice and ducks and squirrels and pigs all gave tiny cheers and waved their paws, webbed feet, and trotters in support.

'OK, comrades,' said Parsifal more loudly, 'this is it! We're going in!'

He puffed out his chest and led his army on wobbly legs up to the enormous marble door of the main hall. This, too, was open. Parsifal was about to peep round the door when he realized that he hadn't told his followers to stop and so, before he could cry 'Halt!', they had all piled up behind him and forced him, skidding, through the doorway. They ended up piled on top of each other (with Parsifal underneath). For a few moments, he had to content himself with hearing the other animals quack and shriek in awed voices before he could battle his way out of the heap.

The rout of the Night Mare's army had obviously taken place here. The doors of the Big Oven were blackened with smoke but were barred shut. In front of them was a broken and twisted mass of metal that Parsifal recognized as the remains of the enormous spit that the Night Mare had used to kill the Big Pig. The long evil skewer was broken into tiny pieces and the supports that had held it up were shattered. Parsifal and the sow looked at each other in amazement. Who could have done this? And what had happened to the body of the Big Pig?

The sow saw him first. She had been about to burst into tears again at the thought of the Big Pig's death, when she saw something at the other end of the enormous room that caused her to catch her breath. She prodded Parsifal with her trotter to take a look too.

There sat the Big Pig, in a cosy armchair with his trotters on a footstool next to a magnificent marble fireplace in which a merry fire was crackling. He was sipping a glass of something and reading a book. He looked up at them and smiled as if everything were perfectly normal.

The shock paralyzed Parsifal for a moment. Then he shot forward like a pig from a cannon and ran to where the Big Pig was sitting. He fell on the marble floor at the Big Pig's trotters and kissed them and bowed low in worship. The sow and the other animals followed his example, even though they weren't entirely sure what was going on.

'Are you alive?' gasped Parsifal. 'Is it really you?'

'You're not a ghost, are you?' said the sow in a frightened whisper.

'Oh no, no, no,' laughed the Big Pig. 'I'm not a ghost. I'm flesh and blood, as you can see. Go on, touch me. Here are the marks of the skewer in my arms and legs. Oh, and here's the mark from that particularly nasty fork that the Night Mare thrust into my side.'

The sow reached out a trotter and gently touched the scar on the Big Pig's left arm. Then she burst into tears. 'Oh, I'm s...s...so sorry that you had to give your life for me because I was s...s...such a silly and senseless pig, and I'm so glad that you're alive and well and that I can s...s...see you again ... oh! I don't know why I'm crying ... I don't know whether it's because I'm happy or sad!'

The Big Pig tenderly wiped her tears with his trotter. Her tears glistened like rainbow drops on his injured arm.

Parsifal was having a hard time taking all this in. 'How ... how ... how...,' was all he could say when he eventually opened his mouth.

'You want to know how I did it?' smiled the Big Pig. 'How come I'm alive when you saw me killed? Well, I'll tell you. The Night Mare had nothing on me. She might have been able to kill me, but she couldn't keep me dead. The Great Farmer knows that I have never done anything wrong and that my destiny is not the Big Oven. When I gave my life in exchange for others, death had no power over me. I was free to take my life back up again. I gave my life in exchange for all animals everywhere so that all of you can be with me and the Great Farmer on the Perfect Farm for evermore!'

'So there really is a Perfect Farm!' cried Parsifal.

'Of course there is!' the Big Pig laughed. 'Where do you think I come from? And I promise there's a sty and a stable and a pond and a cosy hole there for each one of you if you follow in my tracks.'

At that all the animals cheered and began to clap their paws, webbed feet, and trotters and they began to sing and dance.

Parsifal and the sow were about to join in when she suddenly stopped, in pre-jig position, and asked, 'But what about the—you know—Night Mare?'

Parsifal, also with one trotter poised to commence the dance, looked round at the Big Pig. The Big Pig laughed and pointed down at the floor. Parsifal and the sow looked down and saw that the Big Pig's chair and footstool were planted firmly on a hairy black rug. It was the hide of the

Night Mare! Parsifal and the Lady Sow jumped up and down on it a bit for good measure.

'And where's the rest of her ... it ... whatever?' asked Parsifal.

The Big Pig pointed to the tall door barring the way to the Oven that Burns Forever.

The sow grabbed Parsifal's arm and the two of them twirled round on the marble dance floor with the other animals. An orchestra began to play. It was composed of stoats and weasels who had been in the Night Mare's army but who had now been freed from their slavery.

As they danced round the room, Parsifal and his Lady discovered that they were in evening dress. Parsifal was in a penguin suit and black tie, and the sow was resplendent in a white satin dress with leg-of-mutton sleeves. Parsifal had never felt such deep, pure joy.

'If you don't mind my asking,' said Parsifal. 'What's your real name?'

The sow blushed and looked down. 'Primrose,' she replied with a shy smile.

'Primrose!' Parsifal repeated with a satisfied sigh.

Primrose Pig. Parsifal and Primrose. Primrose and Parsifal. It was meant to be. He kissed her gently on her newly pink snout.

And seeing as Parsifal was in his smartest black suit and Primrose was in a lovely white dress, Parsifal asked her there and then if she would be his wife. She instantly agreed and the two of them were immediately married by the Big Pig himself in the now renamed Palace of Pure Delights.

The loving couple danced long into the night, until they found that they were no longer dancing in the ballroom of

It was meant to be

the palace. They were back in the changing room of the
health farm (or, rather, not back there for Primrose, as she
had never been there before).

'Wow!' said Parsifal. He almost fell over with surprise.
'What are we doing here? Perhaps it was a triple or
quadruple dream after all!'

'Don't you mean a quadruped dream?' said Primrose in confusion. 'And how did I get here?'

'I don't know. You must really be the Pig of my Dreams! You stepped out of my dreams and into my arms!'

Primrose giggled—perhaps from shyness, perhaps from embarrassment that the boar in her life could be so corny. But as she looked down she saw something that made her cry out with surprise. For there, beneath their trotters, was a black horsehair hearth rug.

18

The Final Enemy

Some years later, Parsifal was standing in the changing room again.

He was now probably the fittest pig the health farm had ever seen. He was looking at himself in a mirror that filled an entire wall. He had been on so many missions that he was no longer afraid of doing a 'show-and-tell' about the huge change in his life. His 'before-and-after' photos had become the stuff of legend. In fact, so many animals had wanted to join the health farm as a result of his example that more health farms had had to be built. The Catechism Cat had given Parsifal an important role in all this—much to his amazement, as he had always assumed the cat didn't like him. But he had come to realize that she was just as tough and gruff with everybody.

It was the story of how the Big Pig had given his life to save Parsifal that really moved the animals he spoke to on missions—that and the fact that the Big Animal had conquered death on behalf of all of them so they could live for ever with the Great Farmer on the Purrr...er, Perfect Farm.

And now Parsifal was getting to be an old boar. As he looked in the mirror in the changing room he could see grey bristles amongst the black ones—in fact there were probably more grey than black ones now. He and Primrose had had many baby piglets, all of whom had now grown up and gone to help build other health farms. Parsifal and Primrose were very proud parents.

Parsifal looked at himself in the mirror on the wall with great contentment. His own 'before-and-after' still amazed him sometimes. He could hardly recall the Parsifal that had stared back at him from his bedroom mirror in his house that day long ago when he had first seen his need to get fit.

Parsifal smiled to himself and was about to walk away from the mirror, wondering what there was for lunch, when an unpleasant voice called out, 'Hey, you!'

Parsifal turned round. But there was no one else in the changing room. He shrugged his shoulders and headed for the door. But then the same nasty voice cried out, 'Hey you, Fatso! Yes, I'm talking to you!'

Parsifal spun round to see who could be calling him names. And, to his amazement, he came face to face with ... his own reflection.

It was standing there defiantly, as if it had a life of its own. Trotters on hips, it was staring straight at Parsifal with its lips curled in a kind of sneer.

'So, you think you're pretty good now, don't you?' said the reflection. 'But don't worry, you'll always be Slobbo to me. You and I know the truth about you, don't we?'

'Who ... who are you?' gasped Parsifal. '*What* are you?'

'Me? You mean you don't recognize me? Do you need glasses or something? I'm *you!* I'm your flesh. I'm the old little pig you used to love and cherish.'

'But ... but,' Parsifal stammered in horror, 'I've got rid of you! I don't follow the ways of the flesh anymore. I'm not a slob!'

'Ha!' cried the reflection. 'You may not feed me as much as you used to, but that doesn't mean I'm not still around. I'm you, you see. I'm part of you. You'll *never* be rid of me.'

And the reflection broke out in a grating cackle, a parody of the way Parsifal used to laugh when he was a little pig. Parsifal began to despair. But then, as he looked at his cackling reflection, he noticed the words on the T-shirt that he was wearing. It was as if the words were highlighted in yellow fluorescent pen so that even a pig under stress would notice them. Seen backwards in his reflection in the mirror, it read: '!EMOC OT EFIL EHT'. The right way round it read: 'THE LIFE TO COME!'

'What about the life to come?' Parsifal asked his reflection. 'What about that? You said I'll never be rid of you. But what about in the life to come?'

'Huh!' sneered his reflection—though not quite as confidently as before. '"The life to come"? Where did you pick up that fairy story? I know you're a nursery story character, but that doesn't mean you have to believe everything you read. I can't believe you're giving me that old "sty-in-the-sky when you die" nonsense.'

'It's not nonsense!' declared Parsifal stoutly. 'The Big Animal told me about it. The Big Pig promised I would have a place on his Perfect Farm with him and the Great Farmer.'

'The Big Animal? Ha! You can't believe everything he says,' Parsifal's reflection retorted.

But that was a big mistake.

'You're telling me,' said Parsifal, 'to doubt the word of the Big Animal? You're telling me not to believe his promises to me? The one who gave his life for me and rose from the dead?'

'Oh, er, erm,' said his reflection, seeming to grow a bit fainter. 'No, no of course not. I'm just trying to get you to see sense, that's all. No, I've no doubt at all that you're going to die one day, just like the Big Animal. It's what happens to you afterwards that concerns me.'

'Oh?' said Parsifal in spite of himself. 'And what do you mean by that?'

His reflection grew clearer again and pointed to the right-hand wall of the changing room.

'You see that door there?' it asked casually. 'The one marked "EXIT"?'

'Ye-ees,' said Parsifal warily.

'Well that, my fat friend, is where you're headed. Straight out of here, all nice and meaty and juicy, ready to be skewered and cooked in the slaughterhouse next door. Or didn't they tell you about that when you came in here?'

A streak of horror ran through Parsifal's bacon. Slaughterhouse? What slaughterhouse? Surely they hadn't been getting him fit and healthy and happy just to slaughter him?

And yet, as he looked round in desperation, he knew that he had never seen anyone return who had walked out that exit from the health farm. Had his time come to leave? He thought of his wife and children. How could he possibly leave them behind? Even if they were going to join him later, the thought of leaving them even for a little while was unbearable. What was he to do?

Then everything began to happen in slow motion. As Parsifal Pig stood looking at the door marked 'EXIT' he saw the Catechism Cat standing there. Instead of her pink headband, she was wearing black armbands and a big black top hat with a black chiffon scarf round it that billowed out behind her as if she were standing in a breeze. The breeze was coming from the door marked 'EXIT', which was slightly open. Or, rather, the breeze was drawing her scarf towards the door, as if there was a force on the other side sucking everything towards it.

The Catechism Cat raised her paw and waved. 'Goodbye, Parsifal Pig. It's been good to know you. You're ready to go now.'

Parsifal looked round, and there behind him stood his wife, his many children, and the huge crowd of friends he had made at the health farm over the years. They, too, were waving goodbye, and many, particularly his family, were snuffling into handkerchiefs as they said their last farewell.

Parsifal wondered if he should be crying too, when suddenly harsh laughter from his reflection shattered his thoughts.

'Ha, ha, ha, ha!' his reflection crowed. 'And you thought it was going to be easy. Don't you know that this is the final enemy? Death is the final enemy, and now you've got to walk through that door, where you'll fall into the abyss of eternal flame and be cooked for evermore!' And the crazy laughter of his reflection went on and on.

But it was so over the top that, although Parsifal was afraid at first, he came to his senses and had rather an important thought. 'Er, excuse me,' he said to his reflection. 'What happens to *you*, might I ask, if I go through that door?'

His reflection stopped laughing. 'Er, erm...'

'Come on, stop stalling.'

'Well,' the reflection's voice sank to a whisper. 'I have to go too. I'm completely destroyed. You'll never see me again.'

'I thought you said I could never be rid of you,' said Parsifal indignantly.

'Er ... well, I was lying.'

'Too right!' cried Parsifal. 'I don't think I believe anything you say. I'm going to believe my friend the Big Animal who gave his life for me and promised me a home with him for evermore. I believe his word that beyond that door is eternal life with him on the Perfect Farm and that I'm going to be happy with him for ever. So there!' Parsifal stuck his tongue out at his reflection.

'Don't do it, don't do it,' whimpered the reflection. 'You'll kill us both!'

'My body may die, but I won't,' said Parsifal. 'If beyond that door is life for ever with the Big Animal, then that's where I'm headed. And you're not going to stop me. If I get rid of you in the process, then that's just a bonus as far as I'm concerned. You know, I think the only enemy I have left is you!'

His flesh in the mirror shrieked as Parsifal turned to face the door marked 'EXIT'. The sweat was standing out on his forehead, but he gritted his teeth and repeated, 'Remember you are loved, remember you are loved' as he took a step towards the door.

As he did so, Parsifal suddenly saw, illuminated on the ground before him, the trotter-prints of his great friend the Big Pig. They were like rainbow-coloured stars, leading him to the door and beyond. His friend and saviour had gone before him! If following the Big Pig meant going through the door of death, then Parsifal was determined to do it.

Ignoring his protesting flesh, Parsifal Pig stuck his trotters in his ears and ran towards the door, crying out 'I am loved, I am loved, I am *loved!*'

In a moment he was gone. The door closed. No one in the health farm saw him again.

Outside the walls of the health farm, however, there was a grubby street rat (not the street rat who had rescued Parsifal, but another one). He had managed to drag himself out of the city's sewers and had made it as far as the doors of the health farm. He was just slinking away after being thrown out by the Catechism Cat. He had got the answers to the great questions in the catechism hopelessly wrong. He had never met the Big Animal in any shape or form and didn't have a clue about what to do next. The Catechism Cat had told him to try again after something very mysterious happened to him. But that hadn't helped him much. How would he know when something very mysterious had happened to him? And how would he know it wasn't just because he had drunk too much—ahem—cough medicine?

So the street rat mooched around for a while in a bad temper before deciding that he might as well give up and go back to the sewer. How could he expect a respectable health farm like that, full of nice clean animals with good behaviour, to take in a filthy old rodent like him? The street rat groaned and banged his head against the wall. He hated himself so much he didn't know what to do. Maybe he should just go back to the sewer and drink himself to death, and the sooner the better. Nobody would care. Nobody would even notice.

And so the street rat slunk back down the road that led away from the health farm. At the bottom of the hill, before taking the road back to the city, he turned round for one last look. And it was then that something very mysterious happened.

A strange object flew out of a chimney on the roof of the health farm. The rat rubbed his eyes and ran up the hill again for a closer look. It looked like a Range Rover made of light, flying slowly upwards through the sky. It had wheels of spinning flame and its headlights lit up the sky for miles around! And what's more there was a dog hanging its head out of the window, its ears flapping in the wind. No, wait— the rat rubbed his eyes again. It wasn't a dog—it was a pig.

'But that's impossible,' gasped the street rat out loud. 'I must have hit my head harder than I thought.'

Now the pig seemed to be leaning out and saying something, shouting down to him. But of course the rat, being so far away, couldn't hear. Then something even more mysterious happened.

The exhaust fumes from the celestial Range Rover were forming giant letters in the sky—so large that even a street rat under stress could read them. They said:

REMEMBER YOU ARE LOVED!
P.S. THAT'S ALL YOU NEED TO KNOW (FOR NOW)!

Then both the Range Rover and the letters faded into the distant sky.

The rat sat down with a bump. He blinked. He scratched his head with his dirty claws. He stared into space with his mouth open for a while. Finally he came to a conclusion. Either he'd suffered a nasty concussion, or that erm—ahem— cough medicine earlier on in the day had been too much for him, or something very mysterious had just happened to him.

He was loved? How could that be? And who loved him? The street rat decided to find out. At least now he had something to tell the Catechism Cat.

So the street rat gave his whiskers a bit of a preen and a shake, adjusted his fur so the scars wouldn't show as much, and marched with all the determination he could muster up the hill to the health farm again. Perhaps, he thought, someone there saw the message in the sky. If they knew that he, too, was loved, they might let him in. Surely, he thought to himself, when pigs can fly then anything is possible—even something as very mysterious as love.

I am loved!

19

Waking Up

Parsifal the Pilgrim Pig has been lying under the tree where (if you remember) he fell asleep after eating too much at the beginning of his 'pil-grim-age'. Now it is time for him to wake up. (What? You hadn't forgotten it was all a dream, had you?)

He shakes himself. He looks at his stomach and sees with amazement that the drama of his dreams has made him sweat off all his excess weight! He's the fit pig that he's always wanted to be.

'Thank you, Big Pig,' he says as he stands up, 'wherever you are!'

And Parsifal knows, without a shadow of a doubt, that his next task is to find his lost brother and sister. He has to tell them the truth about the Big Animal and how much he loves them. If it's the only thing Parsifal does before he faces the final enemy for real and wakes up for good on the Perfect Farm, then his life will have been worth living.

But that, as they say, is another story...

A free study-guide to this book
can be downloaded from
the *Pig's Progress* product page at
www.piqfic.com

Lightning Source UK Ltd.
Milton Keynes UK

171291UK00001B/3/P